D1230278

THE VALENTINE VICTIM

Also by Dougal McLeish
The Traitor Game

THE VALENTINE VICTIM

Dougal McLeish

Houghton Mifflin Company
Boston 1969

First Printing W

Library of Congress
Catalog Card Number: 69-12443

Printed in the United States of America

THE VALENTINE VICTIM

1

Corporal Tim Moore, who was in command of the Ontario Provincial Police detachment in the village of Farnham, stared morosely out from the window of his office on the second floor of the town hall. Heavy flakes of wet snow drove hard against the glass, melting as they struck, and gusts of wind rattled the window frames. It was just going on six o'clock and technically still afternoon, but outside it was thick night. The February darkness pressed aggressively against the panes like a besieger seeking entrance. Moore felt that if he opened the window the blackness might roll into the room like fog, extinguishing the light.

Directly beneath Moore's window was a small marble cenotaph bearing the names of the young men of Farnham who had died in two world wars and in Korea. Across a tiny square, bordered with shivering elm trees, lights glowed in the Carnegie Library. Beyond the square was the bowling green, enclosed on three sides by a breast-high cedar hedge and three feet deep in snow. As far as Moore could see, the square and the quiet streets that led into it were deserted. There was not even a parked car in sight.

He looked at his wristwatch. He was due to go off duty at six, but Holmsted was going to be late again. He would come in puffing and blowing and beating the snow from his greatcoat, swearing that the weather had held him up. Moore hunched his heavy shoulders to get the stiffness out of them, took his tunic down from the coatrack and put it on. The double row of multi-colored war service ribbons on the left breast began with the blue, red and white stripes of the Military Medal.

The steam radiator under the window made clanking noises and he reached down and shut it off. He checked the drawers of his filing cabinet to see that they were locked. The top of his desk was bare except for his calendar pad. He glanced at this automatically, knowing what was written there. The page was headed *Tuesday, 14 February,* and beneath this in his own handwriting, "chocolates — Rosie." He took out a ball-point pen and drew a line through the notation. His wife had been pleasantly surprised that he had remembered Valentine's Day this year, but her approbation made him feel a little guilty because he had, in fact, been reminded.

Moore opened the top drawer of his desk and took out his own Valentine. Sick. Something to be thrown away and forgotten. But anger shook him again as he looked at the savage caricature — a great sprawling figure in a bright blue police uniform, looking more like an ape than a man. It wouldn't have mattered if it didn't resemble him so closely, but whoever had sent it had chosen with care. Moore had recognized, as he had been intended to, the round head like a soccer ball, the red face, the slightly bulging eyes and the heavy, squat figure. "To a Rotten Cop" was all it said on the card, printed in block letters.

There ought to be a law against things like that. Hate literature, wasn't it?

He heard Holmsted come into the outer office. The door slammed and there came the sound of boots being stamped to get the snow off them. Couldn't think to do it outside in the hall. Moore hastily stuffed the Valentine into the side pocket of his tunic and did up the button. No point in letting Holmsted see it. He'd roar with laughter and, using the laughter as a cover for his resentment and hostility, would come as close to insubordination as he dared. Listen to the great ox puffing and blowing, would you? Moore stood still and was obscurely gratified to hear Holmsted beating his gloved hands against his greatcoat. He had that young fellow's number, all right. But his satisfaction faded when he looked at the electric clock on the wall. Only one minute past six. Late, but not late enough to make an issue of.

Constable Holmsted poked his face around the door. He was a big blond man, four inches taller than Moore's five foot ten, and fifteen years younger than the corporal. He had a heavy, aggressive jaw, dull eyes and a sort of lumbering insolence in his carriage that made Moore long for a certain sergeant-major he had once known.

"Hi," Holmsted said, taking off his uniform cap and slapping it against his leg. "Not much use you going home tonight. The highway's like a skating rink. We're bound to get at least one major accident before morning. I'll have to get you out of bed, I expect."

Moore opened his mouth to snarl a reply, but shut it again.

Behind Holmsted the door of the outer office pushed open. In the doorway, looking in a little uncertainly, stood Mrs. Lori Weston.

Corporal Moore knew her to see her. She was the wife of Dr. Weston, the biochemist who headed the Thameside Laboratories in London and who lived in the big house on Maple Street near the east end of town. Moore thought that Mrs. Weston was probably the most beautiful woman he had ever seen in his life. This afternoon she wore a white fur coat with a matching fur hat and muff and knee-high white boots. The snowflakes were still melting on the fur and on her bright golden hair and dark eyelashes.

Lori Weston smiled at the corporal. It was not the formal smile, polite but distant, that beautiful ladies might be expected to give to strange policemen. Rather it was warm and real, as though she had known him for years, liked him and was glad to see him. Moore stood up straight and brushed past the constable.

"Good afternoon, Mrs. Weston. Won't you come in? What can I do for you?"

Suddenly the comic Valentine seemed unimportant. Moore felt like a man who had authority vested in him, strong, competent, experienced and kindly, not a shambling ape in uniform. Constable Holmsted lounged in the doorway, staring at their visitor as though he had never seen a woman before. When Moore glared at him, he moved aside, going into the inner office.

Mrs. Weston came in, accepted the chair that Moore quickly drew up for her, and sat down. The corporal caught the merest suggestion of some perfume, faint but haunting, like a breath of ever-after. Mrs. Weston crossed her legs and undid her coat.

"No, thank you, I won't take it off. I'll only be staying a few minutes. This is a terrible time for me to come bothering you." She glanced at a tiny gold wristwatch. "Why, it's six o'clock! I expect you're ready to go off duty and that I'm keeping you from your dinner."

Moore hastily denied this, confirmed in his good opinion of her. Most people who came to the police station were so taken up with their own troubles that they never gave a thought to anything else.

She took a thin gold cigarette case from her muff, offered it to the corporal and selected a cigarette for herself. Moore fumbled in his pocket for his lighter, held the flame for her and then walked heavily around his desk and sat down. Uninvited, Holmsted took a chair in the corner of the room.

Under the white fluorescent tubes that lit the inner office, Mrs. Weston did not look quite as young as Moore had thought her to be. If anything, though, she seemed even more beautiful. Thirty perhaps, he guessed, looking with wonder at her face. There were tiny laughter lines at the corners of her gray-green eyes and her high cheekbones and slightly hollowed cheeks gave her a fragile, fine-spun look.

"I would have telephoned you about this," Mrs. Weston said, "instead of troubling you at your office, but my husband has a heart condition and I didn't want to worry him. I was going by here this afternoon in any case, so I thought I'd drop in."

"That's what we're here for," the corporal said. "Any time."

Mrs. Weston blew out a thin blue cloud of cigarette smoke and narrowed her eyes as though she was marshaling her thoughts.

"There isn't much to it really," she said slowly. "Or, so I thought until last night. But it really does look as though someone tried to force the window."

The corporal shifted in his chair.

"Perhaps, Mrs. Weston, if you would just begin at the beginning," he suggested, as he had a hundred times before. "Take your time and tell me the story in your own words."

"It started last week," said Mrs. Weston. "Let's see. This is Tuesday, the 14th. It would have been on Thursday night. The 9th. My stepdaughters were coming home from bridge at Madge Dobson's. It was only two blocks away, so they didn't take the car. About eleven o'clock it would have been. Not really late, but the night was dark. Almost as dark as it is tonight. I was sitting up reading a book when they came in. I saw right away that something had upset them."

She paused for a moment. Corporal Moore sat still and said nothing. He had had a lot of experience with witnesses. Mrs. Weston continued.

"It wasn't much, at least not the way they told it. A man followed them home. Keeping in the shadows so they couldn't see his face. He didn't try to speak to them or anything like that, but when they went inside the house, he crossed the street and stood there, watching the front door."

"Did you see him yourself then?"

"No. When they told me what had happened, I went to the front door and looked out, but if there was anybody there I couldn't see him. The streetlights are shamefully far apart in our area and the one that is nearest to our house is at the corner, a good fifty yards away. If we don't have our verandah light on, the roadway is pitch black, and if we do have the light on, you can't see across the road. Unless you stand in the living room, that is, and turn off all the lights there. I didn't think to do that."

"You say your stepdaughters were upset?" Moore asked. "How old are they?"

Mrs. Weston gave a little laugh.

"Too old to be my daughters. Aileen is twenty-four and Ann is twenty-one. They're not children, if that's what you were thinking. As to their being upset — well, yes, they were. Certainly Ann was. Perhaps she's the more highly strung of the two. And then when it happened the second time —"

"This man turned up again?" Corporal Moore sat up and looked sharply across the desk.

Mrs. Weston nodded. "On Sunday night. Ann was coming home from church at about nine o'clock. She was alone because Aileen was dining in London with her fiancé. The same man — at least I suppose he was the same man — began to follow her as soon as she turned off Main Street. The poor girl was almost running by the time she got to the house and let herself in."

"She didn't get a good look at him?"

"No. It was the same as the first time. He kept well back and in the shadows. Ann said that he had his hat pulled down over his forehead and a scarf or something covering the lower part of his face. Almost like a mask. That was what frightened her most of all, I think."

Corporal Moore looked embarrassed. "I hope you'll pardon my suggesting it, Mrs. Weston, but isn't it possible that your stepdaughters were mistaken? Nothing seems to have happened. The girls weren't approached or molested in any way."

"And that, of course, is why I haven't been here before now, Corporal." Lori Weston's smile took any possible sting out of the words. "But last night somebody tried to break into our house through the kitchen window. I heard him myself. It was about ten o'clock, and Bob had already gone up to bed. Both the girls were out, and I was sitting by myself in the back parlor. Suddenly there came a crash of breaking glass from the kitchen and the sounds of someone trying to force a window open. I jumped up and went over to the fireplace to pick up the poker, then I went out to the kitchen."

Corporal Moore looked as though he had never heard of a braver act. "You shouldn't have," he said softly. "You shouldn't have. It could have been dangerous."

"Well," said Mrs. Weston in a matter-of-fact voice, "it wasn't in the least dangerous as it turned out. There was no one there at all. But a pane in the kitchen window was broken and there were what looked like fresh chisel marks on the outside of the window sash. And there were footprints in the snow outside the window."

"What did you do then?"

"I put a piece of cardboard over the broken pane and went to bed," said Mrs. Weston.

"You should have phoned me. We would have been over in a squad car in two minutes and we might have caught whoever it was."

"Yes," agreed Mrs. Weston. "I certainly thought of that.

But, as I told you, my husband is not well. He had a serious heart attack about six months ago and the doctor warned me that he should never be allowed to become excited. If I had called you and you had come to the house, he would have certainly found out about it. So I decided to say nothing, but to come around and tell you today when I was on my way to Molly Fitzpatrick's Valentine party."

"Have you told your stepdaughters about this incident last night?"

"No. I haven't yet. Ann has been badly frightened twice in the past week, and I saw no point in worrying her further. Besides, the only time I saw the girls was at breakfast and my husband was there too. I told them I had broken the pane myself, trying to open the window."

She stopped and looked expectantly across at the corporal.

Moore began to get out of his chair. "Suppose we go out to your place now and have a look at this window?"

Mrs. Weston shook her head. "I'd rather you didn't, Corporal, if you don't mind. Aileen and Ann are home, dressing for Mrs. Fitzpatrick's party, and Dr. Weston will be arriving back from London any time. No, I only told you all this in the hope that you could—well, keep an eye out. Perhaps your patrol car could drive by Maple Street a couple of times a night for the next little while." She paused and again her green-gray eyes narrowed in thought. "Or if there are any strangers in town —" She broke off.

"I haven't heard of any, Mrs. Weston. And I probably would have. Farnham's a small place. Why do you think it might be a stranger? We've got some poor types right here in town."

Young punks, he thought to himself. Speeding. Driving while impaired. Probably hopped up on junk or LSD. Sending people comic Valentines.

Mrs. Weston did not answer immediately. She seemed to be considering the corporal's words carefully. At last she said, "No, I don't think the man the girls saw could be from Farnham. Both Aileen and Ann have lived here all their lives. Don't you think that even in the dark they would have been able to recognize something about whoever it was who was following them? The walk, the way he carried himself? Something?"

"They didn't?" asked Moore.

A shadow of uncertainty crossed the beautiful face, but very briefly. Then Mrs. Weston shook her golden curls. "No. No, they had no idea at all who it could be."

"And yourself, Mrs. Weston? Have you any idea why anyone would act like this — following the girls home and trying to break in? Always assuming, of course, that it was the same man."

"Of course it was the same man. This sort of thing doesn't happen in Farnham, does it? And when it does — three times in the one week — you can be sure that a single person is behind it."

"I'd say you were certainly right, Mrs. Weston. And you have no idea who might be doing it?"

"None whatsoever. But both Aileen and Ann are young, you know. And attractive. They're both engaged to be married. I thought perhaps it was someone who had seen them in London — they used to work there until a few weeks ago — and that he — whoever it was — had —well — got a crush on one of them. On Ann probably."

"Why on Ann?"

Mrs. Weston looked slightly put out. "She's the younger, I suppose. And perhaps the more attractive to men. And she was followed twice to Aileen's once. I don't know."

Mrs. Weston began to put on her gloves. Incredibly small gloves they were, the corporal thought, looking down at his own huge and hairy hands.

"You may rest assured," he said, using the form of words he often used and liking the sound of them, "you may rest assured we will do all we can. If there's any stranger in Farnham I'll find out about it, and I'll see that a special watch is kept on your street. But I must ask you that if anything else occurs — anything at all — you will let me know immediately. I don't want to alarm you unnecessarily, Mrs. Weston, and in fact I don't think you have any real cause for alarm, but this sounds as though it might be the work of a nut — of someone who is not quite right in the head, I mean. Not dangerous, I wouldn't think, but the sooner we pick him up the better."

Mrs. Weston stood up and held out a white-gloved hand.

"Thank you so much, Corporal. Corporal Moore, isn't it?" Her smile and her ennunciation of his name caused the blood to mount in Moore's red cheeks. "I'm sure we are in safe hands." She looked up at the clock on the wall and gave a little exclamation. "My goodness! Is that clock right? I've been here longer than I intended. I promised Molly I'd be there to help her at six and now it's already twenty past! I must run!"

She turned and left the office. Corporal Moore had to hurry to open the outer door for her. She smiled at him again. "Good-bye now. And thank you."

Moore watched her go lightly down the stairs and out into the darkness. A trace of her perfume lingered in the air behind her. Holmsted loomed up in the doorway of the inner office. His rather vacuous face leered down at the corporal and his pale blue eyes had a gleam in them.

"Now that's what I call a neat bit of goods," he said. "A real neat bit of goods. She could park her shoes under my bed anytime. Eh, Corp?"

"Don't call me 'Corp,'" Moore snapped, "and what's more, Constable —"

He was interrupted by the ringing of the telephone on his desk. He strode over and put his hand on it. "Don't go away," he said over his shoulder. "I want to talk to you."

Then he picked up the receiver.

2

INSPECTOR JOHN RODERICKS was thinking about his dinner. It would, he knew, be beefsteak and kidney pie tonight, with the biscuit crust that his wife made so well. Sweet pickles on the side and a bottle — perhaps two bottles — of India Pale ale. Then, after they had stacked the dishes in the dishwasher, they would sit on either side of a bright coal fire to read and chat desultorily until it was time to go to bed. The two boys would be busy with homework upstairs and their daughter, Mary, would be cramming for her Easter examinations. No need to worry about anyone being out in a car on a night like this. He found himself anticipating the evening's program with a pleasant sense of well being.

He and his secretary had been working late, preparing notes on a murder case that was coming up in the spring assizes. He had three major cases being brought to trial, but although they would require continuous liaison with the crown attorney's office, they were straightforward enough. All the accused were manifestly guilty, and he looked forward with satisfaction to three convictions.

When the telephone rang, he automatically noted the time

— 6:34. He could leave for home immediately after this call.

"Rodericks," he said. "Criminal Investigation Department."

As he listened to the deep booming voice at the other end of the wire, his sense of well being ebbed away. He interrupted his caller.

"Wait a moment please, Corporal." His voice was pleasant — quiet and friendly with no hint of authority in its tone. He flicked the switch of the intercom on his desk. "Joan? Are you still there?"

The intercom crackled back at him.

"Sorry to bother you this late, Joan. But would you see if Sergeant Peele is still in the building, please? If not, try to get him at his apartment. I'd like him here as soon as possible. Yes, we've got another one. You'll have to round up Dr. McCabe. And would you get hold of Sergeant Tapp and Corporal Reid for me, too? They'll probably have gone by now. Have them report to the Duty Officer right away. I'll go with Sergeant Peele. Tapp and Reid can come along as soon as they get their gear together. If Dr. McCabe is here in time he can go with them. But better lay on an extra car in case he isn't. Where to? Farnham, I'm afraid. Yes. Yes, it is a filthy night, but I'll tell the driver to take it easy. Thank you, Joan."

Rodericks put the telephone receiver back to his ear.

"Sorry, Corporal. I had to organize the fingerprint and photography details and the pathologist. You were able to identify the dead woman yourself? Good. Shot, you said? Multiple wounds and no sign of a weapon?"

The booming voice broke in and Rodericks listened in silence until it finished.

"I see," he said. "No description of this man that we can use, eh? Well, I'll put out a check on all known molesters and be with you as soon as I can. The third turn on the right after I pass the village sign. Straight on for four blocks, then turn left. The second house on the left. Yes, I've got it. Good-bye now."

He hung up and stood for a moment in thought, checking over the routine to make sure he had forgotten nothing. He was a very broad and thick-set man in his early fifties, with brown hair that was beginning to be sprinkled with silver and a hard face that was creased with many tiny wrinkles. His cold gray eyes were watchful and shrewd, and when he smiled he looked sly as though he was waiting for the world to lie to him. No one could mistake him for anything but what he was — a police officer of many years' service. He sat down at his desk again and picked up the telephone. He spoke to the Duty Officer, to Records and to the Communications Room. While he was talking, Sergeant Peele came in and shut the door behind him. He was a tall fair man of about thirty, immaculate in a well-cut civilian suit, who looked more like an army officer in mufti than a policeman. Rodericks waved him into a chair. His secretary buzzed him on the intercom as soon as he had finished his final call.

"Sergeant Tapp and Corporal Reid are on their way," she reported. "Dr. McCabe isn't at home or at his office, but I'll keep trying. And your car is ready."

"Good girl. Tell them I'll be down in a minute." He picked up the telephone again, but before he dialed he turned and spoke to Sergeant Peele. "A murder in Farnham, Sergeant. A young woman shot. I'd like you to come along with me, if you don't mind."

"Glad to," said Peele. He looked pleased. He and Rodericks were not a homicide team, for the O.P.P. did not use the team system, but he had often worked with the inspector before. He listened while Rodericks explained to his wife that he would not be home for dinner and that he probably would not be home that night at all.

Rodericks shrugged into his overcoat, drew on a pair of gloves and snapped out his desk lamp. From a steel locker in the corner of the room he took a small overnight bag which he always kept packed and ready. It contained toilet articles, pajamas, underwear, socks and two shirts wrapped in cellophane. He carried it over to the desk and unzipped it. Opening a desk drawer, he took out a paperback book which he stuffed into the top of his bag. Sometimes he was away a week or more on calls like this and he liked to read himself to sleep. He found that paperback classics fitted his requirements admirably, especially if the authors belonged to the romantic school. A year or so before, when an evangelical minister at Craigalachie had killed his wife and attempted to burn her body in the church furnace, Rodericks had been able to get through the whole of Anthony Hope's *The Prisoner of Zenda* while waiting for the case to break, and the bizarre affair of the poisoned widow at Parkhill would always be associated in his mind with Bram Stoker's *Dracula*. The book he had recently been saving against an out-of-town trip was Tolkien's *The Return of the King*. He had never heard of Tolkien or the famous trilogy, *The Lord of the Rings,* until his daughter had bought him a set for Christmas. Then he had devoured the first two books but, like a schoolboy who saves the last candy at the bottom of the bag, he had prudently set the final volume aside for an occasion like this. Perhaps in Farnham, if events did not move too quickly, he would have a chance to return to the Land of Mordor, where the shadows lie, to share the company of Frodo, Gandalf and the Lady Galadriel.

A police car was drawn up in front of the headquarters building. As soon as the uniformed driver behind the wheel saw Rodericks, he began to get out but was waved impatiently back. The inspector scrambled in unassisted and Sergeant Peele followed him.

The storm was keeping most people off the streets. London, Ontario, which is a fair-sized city, seemed to grow smaller as it drew inward to withstand the storm. Here and there a pedestrian hurried by with his head down against the wind, and a few cars crawled along, their headlight beams refracted and splintered by the driving sleet. The streetlights seemed to shed no radiance beyond their immediate vicinity. Along the glistening dark roadway each lamp on its standard was a little blob of glowing yellow, like a lollipop on a stick. The wind shrieked down the street, driving before it great sheets of freezing rain. Inside the car it was stifling hot, but neither the heat that beat up against the windshield nor the rhythmic thrust of the powerful wipers could keep the glass clear. Even before he reached the outskirts of the city the driver had to pull off to the roadside and chip away the obscuring ice with a red plastic scraper.

On the highway the driving was worse, if anything. The trip from London to Farnham normally took no more than half an hour, but tonight they had to creep along at twenty. Rodericks estimated that it would be nearly eight before they reached their destination. Fortunately, there was hardly any traffic on the highway and what there was proceeded cautiously. Cars slowed almost to a walking pace when meeting one another. Near the village of Lucan a huge moving van was lying on its side in the ditch, its eighteen giant wheels still spinning slowly in the air. A provincial police cruiser was already at the scene and portable electric flares had been set up by the roadside to warn other drivers.

Rodericks turned to the sergeant. Although his face habitually wore an expression of almost unnatural stillness and calm, his gray eyes sometimes twinkled with a deceptive merriment. He twinkled at Peele now, but the sergeant knew that this was merely a mannerism, like Lenin's perpetual, silent laughter, and that it did not indicate either amusement or good nature.

"I'd better put you in the picture," Rodericks said. "It won't take long for I don't know much myself. A young woman by the name of Aileen Weston has been found shot in her own home. Her sister discovered the body. There seems no doubt that it was murder. An interesting fact is that at six o'clock, at about the time the murder was being committed, the girl's stepmother was actually at the police station, complaining about a strange man who has been following the two girls around for the past week."

Sergeant Peele frowned. "I don't like the sound of that," he said. "Psychos are hard to catch."

Rodericks grunted. "It's too early to say, but you could

well be right. There's no description, but Records is running through the cards. They may come up with something. Or then again they may not."

"Guy in Winnipeg," said Peele. "Killed three little boys before he was picked up. He had no previous convictions."

"We may be lucky. Our man may be waiting for us when we get there, weeping and remorseful and saying he didn't mean to do it. Ready for you to take down his life story."

"Was she raped?"

"There was no sign of it, but we'll have to wait for McCabe to tell us for sure."

Peele made no reply and the only sound inside the car was the occasional low mutter of the two-way radio in the front seat. Rodericks glanced sideways at the sergeant. One of the things he liked about him was that he did not talk too much. Whenever possible, he took Peele with him on the difficult jobs, partly because he was good at detail, meticulous and hard working, but partly too because his wife had died a year ago and he needed to be kept busy. Anything must be better than going home at night to an empty apartment, Rodericks thought. For a moment the images of the lost beefsteak and kidney pie, the beer, and the coal fire made him wonder if retirement would be so bad after all.

Twice more the driver had to stop to scrape ice from the windshield and side window. They were traveling through a dark countryside whose features were obscured by the night and the storm. The prosperous-looking farmhouses that Rodericks knew were on either side of the road were no more than little patches of mellow light. They passed a few clumps of naked woods and a village that consisted of only a post office, a general store and a railway station.

At five past eight they saw a white sign by the roadside that said:

WELCOME TO FARNHAM
POP. 3,072
DRIVE SLOWLY
SPEED CHECKED BY RADAR

The first houses were half a mile farther on.

Farnham was well over a hundred years old. Until recently it had been populated chiefly by retired farmers and a few shopkeepers, but in the past ten years more and more people who worked in London had bought homes there and commuted daily to and from the city. The main street was the highway, which ran straight as a die through the mile-long village. They passed a few straggling frame houses, crossed a steel-girded bridge over a tiny frozen stream, and then suddenly the houses were larger, closer together, and built of brick or stone. Big maple and chestnut trees, bare and shiny with ice, towered up against the dark sky. There were half a dozen stores closed for the night but with lighted windows, a white brick church with a tower, and a stone mason's yard filled with ice-covered marble angels and glittering granite tombstones. The driver turned off the highway and at once took his foot from the accelerator, for the side street was sheer glare ice. They found themselves in a residential area of huge old houses set well back from the sidewalk and surrounded by spacious grounds. Turning in accordance with Rodericks' instructions, the driver found Maple Street without difficulty.

As soon as they rounded the corner they could spot the house where the murder had been committed. It was a large building of weathered red brick, and light shone from every one of its numerous windows. Outside the house, drawn up barely off the road, were three Provincial Police cruisers, one of which still had its red dome light flashing. They pulled up behind this car and stopped.

Rodericks sat where he was for a moment, with the window rolled down, staring at the house and grounds. Then he gave a little grunt, as though he was reluctant to stir himself, and clambered out. Sergeant Peele followed him up the walk to where Corporal Moore stood waiting inside the glassed-in verandah that ran across the whole front of the house.

3

MOORE STIFFENED TO ATTENTION as the inspector came up the steps. At the verandah door the two middle-aged policemen looked appraisingly at one another. Both men smiled, the merest crinkling of the lines at the corners of their eyes, and the corporal stood back to let Rodericks and Peele go into the house ahead of him.

The front door with its large pane of frosted glass opened into a hall that was furnished with an old-fashioned coat-rack, an umbrella stand, a telephone table with a phone on it, a chair, and a little open closet filled with overcoats and overshoes. A police constable, whom Rodericks recognized as belonging to the Goderich detachment farther up the highway, stood on guard at the end of the hall. He saluted as Moore opened the hall door and motioned the two detectives in.

Rodericks found himself in a large drawing room. A row of windows, covered with drapes of dark-red brocade, looked out on the verandah. On the left was a bay window with similar drapes only half drawn. In the far right-hand corner of the room a curving staircase with a polished bannister made its way heavily but not ungracefully to the second story. Lying at the foot of this staircase, about four feet from the bottom step, was the body of a young woman.

She lay on her back with her arms sprawled out awkwardly at shoulder height, her hands open and the palms up. An overturned chair half covered her feet and lower legs. Rodericks walked over slowly and looked down at her. She was a dark girl in her early twenties, five foot five or so in height and with a good figure. She was wearing an expensive-looking astrakhan coat, unbuttoned, and beneath it a flaming red cocktail dress. Inspector Rodericks went down on one knee beside her.

Her mouth and lower cheeks were badly mangled. Two shots, the inspector thought — one fired almost frontally and one from the left side. The frontal shot had ripped away part of the mouth, broken several teeth and emerged from the right cheek below the cheek bone. The other shot had gone clean through both cheeks, leaving an ugly exit wound with ragged edges.

Bending down close to the dead girl's face, Rodericks peered at the third wound. It was on the left temple immediately below the hairline, a dark red furrow across the upper part of the forehead. This wound had bled freely, for the girl's hair on the left side of her head was matted thick with blood and the left half of her face was splashed with crimson. Rodericks took off his gloves and stuffed them into his overcoat pocket, then he gently lifted a lock of black hair, ignoring the stains that appeared on his fingers. The red furrow petered out above the hairline where the skull curved. The inspector did not believe that any of these wounds would have caused death, unless it were from shock or possibly from loss of blood.

Gently Rodericks opened the girl's coat, and his problem was at once solved. On the left breast, grouped about the heart, were three bullet holes, small dark circles which looked as though they might have been seared in with a hot iron rod. There had been almost no external bleeding. Very delicately Rodericks put a large blunt finger on the girl's breast by the topmost wound. Then he stood up in one easy movement and looked at Sergeant Peele.

"Any of those three shots would have killed her," he said. "They were all fired at point-blank range. With the muzzle of the gun actually touching the body, I should think. You'll notice the powder burns. By the feel of it, her dress is actually fused to her skin."

Sergeant Peele bent over to look. The inspector seemed to be waiting for something.

"She must have been unconscious?" Peele asked.

"Very likely. Not necessarily though. No, that's not what I meant. Look at that wound on the forehead."

Peele looked.

"Well?" said Rodericks.

"Superficial," said Peele. "Would knock her out and would bleed like blazes but she wouldn't die from it."

Rodericks nodded. "She didn't die from it. And she didn't bleed all that much either. At least I don't think so."

Peele waited for him to continue but if he had been going to say more, he apparently changed his mind. He stared down at the dead girl, his face thoughtful but composed. Looking at him, no one would have guessed how bitterly resolved he always was at these times to see justice done.

At last he turned away from the body and looked slowly around the room, taking it in for the first time. It was, he decided, a beautiful room, if you cared for that style — massive mahogany furniture, built as only the Victorians could build, and upholstered in the same dark-red brocade as the drapes, a gorgeous Oriental rug that would have cost as much as his annual salary, two rather somber oil paintings on the walls, an ornate fireplace with logs and kindling laid ready for lighting. Diagonally across the room from the staircase was a pair of French doors standing open. Beside them was Constable Holmsted, looking hulking and uncertain. From the floor above there came faint sounds of men moving about.

"They're making a preliminary search of the house," Moore said in reply to the inspector's look of inquiry. "To see if there are any indications of robbery. And for anything else they can find. If you agree, sir, I'll do it more thoroughly myself later tonight."

"Excellent, Corporal. But who have you got up there?"

"I borrowed three men from Goderich, sir. They were on highway patrol, but I thought I might need all the help I could get."

"Quite right, but we can send them back in an hour or two, I think. My own people will be here by then, and we'll need cars on the highway tonight."

Rodericks moved over to the French doors and Holmsted drew back to let him pass. As the inspector went through into the next room, he noticed out of the corner of his eye that Holmsted's chin was covered with short fair hairs. Obviously he had shaved the previous night rather than that morning, in the belief that he could get away with it because he was so fair. The sight of that light stubble angered Rodericks and he made a mental note to speak to Corporal Moore about it later.

The back parlor was smaller than the drawing room, but was still a good size. In the center of the ceiling half a dozen light bulbs blazed nakedly from a brass chandelier of singular ugliness. Another pair of open French doors led into a gloomy looking dining room and through them Rodericks could see that off the dining room there was a little hall which contained a straight and unpretentious back staircase. The parlor was furnished in the same Victorian style as the drawing room. It contained a love seat with a padded back, a long, slightly curved settee, and three occasional chairs, but the most imposing piece of furniture was a grand piano in one corner. On top of the piano was a photograph in a silver frame. Rodericks walked across to look at it.

He carried it back to the center of the room under the chandelier and put on a pair of reading glasses. He did this reluctantly, for he hated to be reminded that his eyes were not as good as they had been even a few years ago. The picture seemed to be an enlarged snapshot, although a very good one, and it had been taken on the front lawn of the Weston house. There were four people in the photograph, three women and a stout, intellectual-looking man of middle age. One of the women was Aileen Weston. Beside her stood another girl who was somewhat taller, younger and much prettier. This girl bore such an unmistakable resemblance to the man in the photograph that anyone would have recognized them as father and daughter. On the other side of the man was a blonde woman who possessed the ethereal beauty that is sometimes seen in the faces that gaze down from medieval tapestries. A line of poetry came unbidden into Rodericks' mind — "the hollow cheek to drink the wind . . ." Merely looking at her picture made him think of ancient tales, enchantments and high towers by lonely seas.

Still holding the photograph in his hand, he turned to Corporal Moore.

"Where is everybody?" he asked.

Moore's round, red face went a shade redder.

"That's Aileen Weston in there." He moved his head to indicate the drawing room. "Her sister Ann was the one who found her. She's across the street now at a neighbor's. She was hysterical and the doctor had to give her a sedative. The father, Dr. Weston, got home soon after I arrived here. He burst in before Constable Holmsted could stop him. When he saw his daughter dead, he had a heart attack — a pretty bad one by the looks of it. An ambulance took him to hospital. His wife and the doctor are there with him."

As he finished this recital of disaster, Corporal Moore looked straight ahead as though expecting some rebuke, but Rodericks merely said, "You'd better give me the whole story from the beginning."

"Yes, sir." Moore relaxed ever so slightly. "Well, as I told you over the phone, Mrs. Lori Weston — that's the wife, the stepmother of the murdered woman — Mrs. Weston came to our headquarters this afternoon at six o'clock to lodge a complaint about a strange man who had been molesting her stepdaughters."

"Molesting?"

"Well, following about, sir. Not what you could properly call molesting perhaps. Frightening."

"Go on."

"Mrs. Weston left at six-twenty, and a minute or two after she had gone I got a telephone call from Mrs. Middleborough who lives directly across the street from here. Ann Weston had come running over to her place in a great state, saying that her sister had been murdered. Constable Holmsted and I came here at once. We found the front door standing open —"

"That would be the door inside the verandah?" the inspector interrupted. "The one with the frosted glass panel?"

"That's right, sir. The verandah door closes automatically with one of those spring gadgets. We found the front door open and when we entered the house we discovered Miss Weston's body lying where you saw it. Doctor Bannister — that's the Weston's family doctor, sir, and a friend of the family — had arrived before us. Mrs. Middleborough had called him before she phoned the station. The doctor was standing by the body. He had already found there was nothing he could do, you see, and he was waiting for us."

"Were the lights on as they are now?"

"Yes, sir," said Moore. "Nothing has been touched. Everything is just as we found it. Except upstairs and in the kitchen where we had to turn the lights on to search."

He paused but when the inspector made no comment he went on.

"I examined the body, sir, and satisfied myself that it was a clear case of murder. There was no sign of the weapon, but I noticed that the blood on the face of the corpse had not yet congealed. And I thought that there was still a smell of cordite in the room. But I couldn't swear to that last."

"What time did you discover the body, Corporal?"

"It was exactly six twenty-six, sir."

"Good man. And then?"

"Then I left Constable Holmsted to guard the body and went across the street to Mrs. Middleborough's. Dr. Bannister came with me. I telephoned you from Mrs. Middleborough's, sir."

"Did you manage to question the sister at all?"

"Only briefly, sir. She was pretty well incoherent, as I said. Sobbing and shrieking and shaking all over like a leaf. But I did get some of it out of her before the doctor gave her the injection."

Corporal Moore took out his notebook and glanced at it. "While I was waiting for you to come, I made some notes of what was said. According to Miss Ann Weston, both the girls were getting ready to go to a Valentine party. The same one Mrs. Weston was at, only she had started out earlier to help the hostess with some things. Anyway, Ann Weston was downstairs in the back parlor, mending a glove. She was in her slip, as I understand it, and that's why, when the doorbell rang, she ran upstairs to put on a dress and left her sister to answer the door." Moore gave a little shrug with his massive shoulders. "You'll understand, sir, that all this is only what I could piece together, as it were. She seemed almost out of her mind when she was telling it, and I may have got some of it wrong."

"That's all right, Corporal. I shouldn't think you have. Anyway we'll put it all together as we go along."

"Well, Ann Weston saw a shape through the frosted glass of the front door — just the outline of the head and shoulders, I think it must have been. Then she went up to her room to put on her dress. She heard her sister talking in a low voice to someone in the hall and she thought it was probably young Mr. Anstruthers. He is — was — engaged to Miss Aileen Weston. She thought it might be Anstruthers because of the way they kept their voices down, if you see what I mean."

"She didn't recognize Anstruthers' voice?"

"Oh no, sir. Nothing like that at all. It was only what she thought at the time. Then, when she was about ready to come downstairs again, she heard some shots, coming from the drawing room, as we know now."

Inspector Rodericks stirred impatiently at this bit of deduction but said nothing.

"Then there was this terrible scream. A sort of gurgling scream, she said it was, and I can believe it."

"Yes," agreed Rodericks grimly, thinking of the ghastly wounds in Aileen Weston's face. "Yes, so can I."

"She sort of froze for a minute, I guess, sir. Her bedroom door was open and she was part way out in the hall. Then she heard someone start up the stairs. Just the footsteps — heavy like, not hurrying."

Corporal Moore told a story well, Rodericks reflected. He could see in his mind's eye the terrified girl outside her bedroom door, listening to the murderer's footsteps coming slowly up the stairs.

"Well then, sir," Moore went on, "she took off like. Ran down the hall to the back stairs, out through the kitchen and into the backyard. She didn't look back, she said, till she reached the wall at the end of the yard. She was sort of trapped there though, because the wall was too high for her to get over and the only gate was frozen shut and blocked with snow so it wouldn't open. I guess she thought she'd had it then for a bit. But the garden is a big one and that end was all in shadow, so she just stayed there."

"You've no idea how long she stayed there?"

"No sir. And to tell the truth, I don't think she knows either. Probably not long, I should think, for after a while she saw someone crossing the street as though he was going away from the house. No, sir," Moore said quickly to forestall the question he could see was coming, "she couldn't make out who it was. It's terribly dark tonight and the streetlight at the corner's a long way off. All she could see was that it was a man in a hat and overcoat."

"What did she do next?"

"She went back into the house. I don't know how soon. She may have waited a bit longer in the garden first. Most probably she did, I'd think. Anyway, she did go back. Through the kitchen door. And she found her sister. I think she must have had some sort of nervous breakdown then. At least she doesn't seem to remember anything that happened after she saw her sister lying dead on the floor. She had no recollection of going over to Mrs. Middleborough's and when I asked her about it she seemed dazed and confused. But it's easy enough to tell what she must have done — she ran out the front door and across the street to Mrs. Middleborough's."

Rodericks lifted the photograph and stared at the family group again. It always appalled him to see how quickly disaster could strike. When the picture had been taken, it had been summertime in Farnham, for the dwarf hollyhocks in front of the house had been in full bloom. The faces within the silver frame looked back at him, innocent and unknowing. It was hard to tell from a picture, of course, but the dead woman seemed to have a rather petulant expression. Perhaps 'petulant' was not the exact word. Prim perhaps? Almost spinsterish? He walked back to the piano and replaced the photograph.

"Did you happen to notice whether there were any blood stains on Ann Weston's hands or clothing?" he asked. Seeing Moore's startled look, he went on, "She might have taken her sister in her arms, you know. It would have been a natural thing to do."

"No, sir. I didn't see any. Of course, I couldn't examine her, as you might say. But there certainly was no blood on her hands. I couldn't get as much out of her as I'd have liked because Dr. Bannister gave her an injection to quiet her. It must have been a strong one. She passed out right away and the doctor had to carry her upstairs."

"Yes. And then?"

"Dr. Bannister and I came back here, sir." Moore's face took on a wooden expression and his voice went flat. "Dr. Weston had come home by then, and, as I said, Constable Holmsted wasn't able to keep him out of the house. When I got back he was lying on the floor. At first I thought he was dead too, but Dr. Bannister said that it was a bad heart attack but they might be able to save him. He had the ambulance here for him quicker than I would have believed possible. He got right in the back with him and started to give him oxygen on the way to the hospital."

"Quite an evening," said Rodericks. "And where was Mrs. Weston all this time? At the Valentine party?"

"Yes, sir. At Mrs. Fitzpatrick's. I telephoned her there and told her what had happened. I hated to do it, too, I can tell you. Mrs. Weston is a lovely lady. Naturally it was a terrible shock to her, but once she understood what I was telling her, she pulled herself together. She answered me, very quiet and sad, and said that since there was no help that could be given to Aileen she would go right to the hospital to be with her husband."

Rodericks walked back to the drawing room and Corporal Moore followed him. Sergeant Tapp, the fingerprint man, and Corporal Reid, the police photographer, were already there and at work, the one dusting white powder about the room and the other taking pictures as quickly as he could change flash bulbs.

They had done this sort of thing a hundred times before and needed no instructions, so Rodericks left them to it. Taking Moore and Peele with him, he went back to the kitchen. It was a large bright room and, in contrast to the rest of the house, as modern as the latest trade fair. The elaborate electric stove, the refrigerator and the deep freeze unit were built into the wall, as was the infra-red oven. A breakfast nook with a bay window in it was almost a separate room by itself. There was a pantry off to the back, a tiny half-bathroom at the west end of the kitchen, and a door that led down to the basement. By the pantry door was a window with a broken pane of glass which was covered with a bit of cardboard torn from a box of breakfast cereal. Rodericks removed the cardboard and inspected the chisel marks that were visible on the outside of the sash.

"A remarkably amateurish job," he said. "Why should anyone both try to pry the window up with a chisel and also break the pane? Once the glass was broken all he had to do was put his hand in and release the catch."

"Perhaps he tried the chisel first," suggested Moore, "and then, when he found that didn't work, he put his elbow through the window."

"Perhaps," said Rodericks, but without conviction.

Sergeant Peele produced a large flashlight and they all went out to stand on the back porch. Freezing rain was still falling from a black sky but not as heavily as it had been half an hour earlier. The footprints under the broken window led off to the left of the house but they had been too blurred by the storm to be more than faint and shapeless indentations in the snow. Ann Weston's footprints, on the other hand, were still quite distinct. There were two separate sets, one coming and one going, for on her way out of the house she had moved to the right and followed the garden wall, hugging its shadow, while on her way back she had come directly from the gate across the open lawn. Rodericks and Peele followed her course to the end of the garden, moving parallel to her footprints and a few feet away.

The inspector was frowning by the time he got back to the house.

"I want those photographed, Ted — all of them. And Reid had better begin right away. An hour or two more of this rain and there won't be much of them left."

They took off their rubbers on the porch and wiped their feet carefully on the mat in front of the pantry door but they still trailed dampness across the kitchen. When they got back to the drawing room Peele led Corporal Reid away to photograph the footprints and the chisel marks. Rodericks hung up his overcoat in the front hall and then found himself drawn back to the body of the dead girl. He was still staring down at her a few moments later when the hall door opened and a plump little man bustled in.

"Fine goddamn weather you pick for your murders, John," Dr. McCabe said while he removed his overcoat. He stepped across to the body, pursed his lips and shook his head. "Terrible business," he muttered. "Terrible!"

"Can you do the autopsy here?" Rodericks asked. "Or will you have to do it in London?"

"Oh, we'll do it here. One of the local doctors can assist."

"Fine. Better not have Dr. Bannister though. He seems to have been the second person to have seen the body and we'll need him as a witness for that. I'd rather have somebody else."

Sergeant Peele put his head around the hall doorway and spoke in a low voice.

"Dr. Bannister's just got back from the hospital. Do you want to see him now?"

"Indeed I do," said Rodericks briskly. "In the dining room, I think. You had better come in too, Ted."

As he walked away, Dr. McCabe was already on his knees, beginning his examination of the dead girl.

4

RODERICKS SHOOK HANDS with Dr. Bannister and waved him into a chair at the dining room table. Before he sat down the doctor took off his overcoat and scarf and draped them carefully over the back of the chair next to the one the inspector had indicated. Rodericks seated himself at the head of the table. Peele took a seat opposite the doctor and produced his shorthand notebook and pencil. He did not try to hide them but, on the other hand, neither did he draw undue attention to what he was doing. The two policemen looked steadily at their witness.

Dr. Bannister was a tall, well-built man with a pleasant face. Rodericks guessed that he was in his early forties. Now he looked worried and depressed, which was only natural in a family doctor who was also a family friend.

When Rodericks spoke he did not refer directly to the murder.

"How is your patient?" he asked.

Bannister shook his head gloomily. "If you mean Bob Weston — not good. His condition is critical, but for the moment we have done all we can." Rodericks detected a touch of coldness in his tone.

"I'm sorry to hear it. He had a previous heart condition, I understand?"

"He suffered a severe coronary early last August. A good deal of permanent damage was done. But he was recovering well, I thought, and he might have lived for several years. As it is —" Bannister shrugged, "he may die at any time."

The doctor lifted his head and looked the inspector straight in the eyes. "I may as well tell you," he said, "that I hold the police partly responsible for that."

The lines deepened about Rodericks' mouth. He returned the other man's stare.

"I don't want to be unfair," Bannister went on, "but your constable should never have allowed Dr. Weston to view the body. Those face wounds would have been a terrible shock to any father." He let it go at that, but the inspector could sense his anger.

"It will be investigated," Rodericks said impassively, "and if Constable Holmsted was negligent, appropriate action will be taken."

To himself he thought that Holmsted almost certainly had been negligent, and he shared the doctor's anger. He wondered if Bannister had noticed the constable's unshaven chin. He probably had. He looked like a man who would not miss much. Rodericks pushed this secondary problem to the back of his mind.

"I hear that this house was empty when you arrived, Doctor. Would you be good enough to tell me the whole story, as it concerns you, from the moment you were notified that Miss Weston had been shot?"

Bannister leaned back in his chair and shut his eyes briefly. Then he opened them and began to speak.

"I was in my office when Mrs. Middleborough phoned me. My last patient had gone some time before and so had my nurse. I had stayed on for an hour or so by myself to look at some X-rays, and it had taken me longer than I'd thought. As a matter of fact, I had my hat and coat on and was just leaving when the phone rang. That was at six-twenty by my watch. My watch was right, by the way, for I had set it at noon with the radio in my car."

"Times are often important in a case like this, Doctor," Rodericks said gently. "And so policemen have to pay special attention to them. Have you ever noticed that most people, when you ask them the time, give it to you to the nearest five minutes? They even make watch and clock dials that way now, with the minutes not marked off."

"Very tactful of you to put it like that," Bannister said, a shade impatiently. "Now that you mention it, yes — I was giving you the time to the nearest five minutes. I won't swear to the exact time, but a good guess would be about eighteen minutes past six."

"Thank you, sir. It's probably not important, but you never know. Now can you tell me, as nearly as you can remember, exactly what Mrs. Middleborough said to you?"

"She was very excited. It was a moment or two before I could get much sense out of her." A little smile touched the doctor's face, making him look almost boyish. "You'll see her yourself, Inspector."

Rodericks nodded.

"I finally gathered that Aileen Weston had been shot in her own home. Mrs. Middleborough did not know anything about her condition. Once I established that, I cut her short and came over here."

"You drove?"

"Yes. Although it's only a three minute walk, or less. My car was in the driveway. I didn't want to waste any time. Aileen might have been alive, you know."

"Of course. And then?"

"I pulled up in front of the house and ran up the walk. I found the front door inside the verandah open and I went right in. Aileen was lying as you saw her. Nobody else was here."

"What time would that have been?"

"I didn't look at my watch," Dr. Bannister said, "but only a few minutes — a very few minutes — after the phone call. Two or three at the most, I would say."

"Then six-twenty or six-twenty-one would be a reasonably accurate estimate?" The inspector made a note in a little leatherbound book he took from his pocket.

"It took only a moment to ascertain that there was nothing I could do," Bannister continued. "Death would have been instantaneous."

"From the wounds in the breast, you mean?"

"Yes. The facial wounds and the scalp wound were not the cause of death. It's more your business than mine, Inspector, but I think this murder must have been committed by someone who was overcome by sudden, blind rage. Probably by someone unused to firearms. He emptied his revolver into the girl's body and went on firing until he ran out of ammunition."

"If it was a revolver," said Rodericks. "One naturally thinks of that, of course. Because of the six wounds. But it could have been an automatic pistol for all we know yet. Most of them hold nine shots, not counting the one in the chamber. You didn't see any sign of the weapon, I take it?"

"I didn't look. Not until after the two policemen arrived, that is. My whole attention was concentrated on Aileen. I knew her well, you know, Inspector. It was a terrible shock to me. After the police came, we all searched for the gun — whatever it was. It wasn't there."

"From your examination of the body, Doctor, could you make any estimate as to when death had occurred?"

Dr. Bannister raised his eyebrows.

"Well," he said, "we know that, don't we? Ann Weston actually heard the murder being committed. She heard the shots."

"I haven't spoken to Miss Weston yet," Rodericks reminded him, "but I understand that, according to her story, the shots were fired at about six o'clock. What I am asking you is whether, from your observation of the body, that seems a likely estimate of the time of death."

"Extremely likely, I should say." The doctor's tone was dry. "Blood was still oozing a little sluggishly from the scalp wound. The body was warm. And even more to the point there was still a faint odor of gunpowder in the air. I'm sure you will find Miss Ann Weston a most reliable witness."

"Of course. I wasn't suggesting anything else. I take it, Doctor, that you know all the Weston family well?"

"In a village the size of Farnham everyone knows everyone else, Inspector. Or to be more accurate, I suppose, everyone above a certain level of income knows everyone in the same group. Yes, I've been friends with Dr. Weston for quite a few years. We used to golf together a fair amount before his heart attack. I've known Aileen and Ann for years too."

"Did they have any domestic problems to your knowledge?"

"None at all. Or none in the sense you mean. The girls and their stepmother got along splendidly. I had some doubts when I first heard that Bob Weston was marrying someone little older than his daughters but Lori soon resolved those when I met her."

"So the family was a happy one in every way?"

"Undoubtedly," said Bannister. "Weston's poor health has recently made quite a change in their way of life, of course. That's unavoidable. Before his heart attack, he was a big, active, virile man, more like a business tycoon than a scientist. But, as you probably know, in cardiac cases a certain type of psychosis often develops — a cardiac personality. The patient becomes over-cautious, worries about himself and tends to be preoccupied with his illness. Bob was showing some of those symptoms, but not to any serious degree."

"Did the two girls get along well together?"

"Yes," said Bannister, "I would say so. Aileen was perhaps inclined to play the older sister a little, and this probably made Ann somewhat restive at times. But this problem — if it was a problem — was not serious. They were very fond of each other and took pleasure in each other's company. Ann, I think, relied a good deal on Aileen's judgment."

The doctor broke off and Rodericks had the impression he had checked himself from saying more, possibly because he believed that his position as family physician should impose discretion. There was no need to make an issue of it now. Whatever may have been on Bannister's mind would be known to others who would feel none of the doctor's nicety about professional ethics.

"Since we're speaking of Ann Weston," Rodericks said, "when will I be able to talk to her?"

"Not tonight, that's certain. I had to administer a powerful sedative and I have every hope that Ann will remain unconscious for upward of twelve hours. She was really in a very serious state of shock. If she were awakened now or if any attempt was made to question her prematurely, the results could be most serious."

"A pity," said Rodericks. "We do rather like to interview the principal witness as soon as we can. Especially in a case like this."

"Why especially in a case like this?"

"Because it's possible she might be able to describe the murderer. I understand that she actually saw him."

Dr. Bannister frowned. He looked, Rodericks thought, as though the events of the past few hours had strained his nerves badly.

"Yes, she saw him. She did tell me that much. But she wasn't able to describe him at all. He was just a dim figure in a hat and overcoat crossing the road at some distance from the streetlight."

"Well, since I don't seem able to talk to Miss Weston herself tonight, you had better tell me in your own words everything that happened after you discovered Miss Aileen Weston dead."

"My examination of the body did not take long," Dr. Bannister said slowly. "And now that it comes right down to it, of course, I am really only guessing that the three wounds about the heart were the cause of death. Almost certainly they were, but we won't know for sure until the autopsy. I made no thorough examination and in fact I didn't move the body. I heard the police — Corporal Moore and the constable — come in while I was still on my knees. I got to my feet and turned around to see who it was." He smiled again. "I think we were all a little nervous. I know that when I heard footsteps in the hall behind me, my first thought was that it might be the murderer returning or coming out of hiding somewhere. And I noticed that the constable had his holster flap undone when he came into the room with Corporal Moore right behind him."

"It must have been an uncomfortable moment," Rodericks agreed soberly. "The quiet house with the murdered girl lying at the foot of the stairs. The storm outside . . . What happened next?"

"Moore and I talked together for a moment or two, and then Mrs. Middleborough arrived. She was very excited, and was downright rude to your policemen, but I fancy she would have come over even if Ann had not been having hysterics in her kitchen."

"Curious was she?"

Dr. Bannister made a little face. "She practically pushed past the constable to see the body, and then she was sick."

Rodericks looked surprised. "In the drawing room?" he asked.

"No. She made it to the bathroom off the kitchen, but she was in there for a good five minutes, retching and vomiting."

"You waited for her then? You didn't go over to Miss Ann Weston right away?"

"Sorry, Inspector," Bannister said. "I've misled you. No, I didn't go over until Mrs. Middleborough came out of the bathroom, because it wasn't until then that she told me why she had thrust herself upon us. When she first entered the house she was, as I said, upset and excited and she spoke rather bitterly to Corporal Moore, implying that if he spent less time worrying about minor traffic offenses there would be fewer murders in Farnham. She came rushing in and — well, she took us all by surprise, I think. She had shoved herself past the constable and was looking down at the body before anyone could stop her."

Twice in one night, Rodericks thought to himself. Not a very good record for us. First the Middleborough woman and then the father. One only nauseated but the other almost killed. The first time was understandable — perhaps — but surely after the experience with Mrs. Middleborough there was all the more reason for seeing to it that no one else wandered in to look at the corpse. All this would have to be gone into very thoroughly later on.

"I see. And when she finally came out of the bathroom?"

"She was still pretty green and a good deal less ebullient than she had been. She told me, quietly enough, that Ann Weston was in a bad way and asked me to go to her. She even apologized for not having said this at once."

"And you then went across the street to Mrs. Middleborough's?"

"Yes. Corporal Moore and Mrs. Middleborough came with me. Moore left his constable to stand guard over the body. And, Inspector, what I said earlier on about blaming the police for Dr. Weston's heart attack should not be taken as any reflection on Corporal Moore. He had some telephoning to do — to you, and to get reinforcements here from the next detachment up the highway — and he didn't want to use any of the telephones in this house until they had been fingerprinted."

Bannister paused and rubbed his right hand over the lower part of his face in a gesture of weariness. Rodericks noticed that his hand trembled a little.

"In fact," the doctor went on, "forget the whole thing. The truth is, I'm dead tired and all this has been a bit hard on my nerves. I have no right to blame the constable for what happened. I don't even *know* what happened. But Weston is an old friend of mine. I'm sorry."

"Good of you to put it like that," the inspector said.

It *was* good of him, considering the circumstances. A very fair man apparently, this Bannister. All the same, Constable Holmsted would have some explaining to do. But whatever the outcome of that, it would be better to keep it within the force. Rodericks could be a strict disciplinarian but he hated any outside criticism of his organization.

"What did you find when you got to the Middleboroughs'?" he asked. "Is there a Mr. Middleborough, by the way?"

Bannister shook his head. "She's a widow. What did I find? Well, I found Ann in the kitchen, terrified out of her wits and hysterical. I questioned her briefly and tried to quiet her, but she fainted twice while I was talking to her. The second time that happened I gave her a strong injection of Nembutal and put her to bed in Mrs. Middleborough's spare bedroom."

"You say you questioned her briefly. I'd be glad if you would tell me exactly what was said." Rodericks made a little gesture with his right hand. "It's not evidence, of course. But anything that will give us an early lead on the killer may be vitally important."

"I fully realize that," Bannister said seriously. "Anyone who could do this can't be sane. And if we have a madman on the loose he may kill again. That's what you mean, isn't it?"

Rodericks agreed, a little ponderously, his gray eyes cold and impersonal. Sergeant Peele looked at him sharply, wondering what was going on in his mind. There was something not quite right about the inspector's reaction to that one. Peele could not pin it down, but he was sure the old fox wasn't leveling with the doctor.

Bannister had taken up the story again. It differed in no particular from what they had already been told by Corporal Moore — the ringing of the doorbell, Ann running up the stairs in her slip, leaving Aileen to answer the door, the sound of low conversation in the drawing room.

"Was Miss Weston still in her slip when she ran out of the house?" the inspector asked. "How was she dressed when you saw her at Mrs. Middleborough's?"

"She was fully clothed. That is to say, she had on a cocktail dress and stockings but no shoes, hat or coat. She was thoroughly wet and chilled to the bone. I don't know how long she spent in the garden and neither does she, but it was long enough for the snow to soak through her clothes to the skin. She'll be lucky if she isn't down with pneumonia on top of everything else." He looked thoroughly wretched at the prospect.

"What did she say about returning to the house? It seems a strange thing to do, doesn't it? Why didn't she run around the house to Mrs. Middleborough's, I wonder?"

Bannister suddenly flared up. "That's ridiculous!" he declared angrily. "If you knew Ann, you wouldn't wonder at it for a moment. Her sister was inside the house, wasn't she? Perhaps wounded — in need of help — of course, she would go in to see."

Inspector Rodericks gave a little shrug.

"I didn't mean anything in particular," he said wearily. "No doubt you're right. If so, it was a very brave thing for her to do."

"What do you mean 'if so'? That's the way it happened. When she saw that her sister was dead she ran out the front door and across the street. Mrs. Middleborough said she pounded on her door like a crazy woman."

"It was locked, was it?"

"I don't know. I suppose so. What does it matter?"

"It couldn't matter less. I'm only trying to get the picture of what happened. Is there anything else you can tell me? Anything Miss Weston saw or heard that could help us identify this man?"

"I don't think so. No. She couldn't say whether he was tall or short, dark or fair. She didn't see his face. She can't even tell us the color of his overcoat. Just that it was dark. I asked her all that. And so did Corporal Moore."

"Was she sure that the man came out of this house?"

"She thought so. Yes, I think she was sure of that." Dr. Bannister considered for a moment. "She couldn't have seen him, of course. At least I'm fairly sure she couldn't have. The front door must be hidden from any part of the back garden, I'd say. I'm almost certain that what she said was that she saw the man crossing the street, as though he was going away from the house. He was hurrying, she said. Not running but walking fast. Anyway, Inspector, you can get all this from Ann in the morning. Unless she's sicker than I hope she'll be."

Inspector Rodericks stood up and walked over to the French doors that led to the back parlor. In the drawing room Reid was packing up his camera and equipment; Tapp had already left. Watched closely by Dr. McCabe, two ambulance men were carrying out the body, covered now with a white sheet. The place where it had lain was marked with a thick chalkline on the floor. Rodericks noticed that there was quite a pool of blood, more than he had thought. He was surprised that there was so much blood. He took half a step forward as though to have a closer look, then decided against it. Better finish with the doctor first. He came back and sat down again at the head of the dining room table. Taking an old briar pipe from his pocket, he filled it carefully from a leather pouch, stuffing the shreds of tobacco down with a stubby forefinger. When he had it filled, he decided not to light it after all. Smoking on an empty stomach never agreed with him.

"After you got Miss Weston to bed you came back here?" he asked. Then before Bannister could answer, he added— "Why?"

The doctor gave a lop-sided little grin. "Thorough devil, aren't you? All right. I was sent for again. I seem to have spent a lot of time going back and forth between these two houses tonight. The constable came and fetched me when Dr. Weston collapsed."

"I see." Rodericks' voice was carefully noncommital, his next question entirely neutral in tone. "And when you got back here to attend to Dr. Weston, who was in the house?"

"Just Dr. Weston, Aileen's body, Corporal Moore, the constable and myself."

God Almighty, said Sergeant Peele to himself, won't this sound good from the witness box! After the murder has been discovered the bleeding corpse is left alone in the house except for an unconscious man! That poor sod Holmsted will be skinned alive.

Rodericks showed no sign of being aware of anything out of order. He merely asked in a mild voice what Bannister had done next.

"I gave Weston a nitroglycerine tablet and called for an ambulance. You'll find my fingerprints on the telephone in the hall, by the way, for that's the one I used. The living are more important to me than the dead."

"Very proper too, sir, I'm sure," Rodericks replied. "No time to do anything else, in a case like that."

"That's all really. The ambulance came very promptly. I got Weston under oxygen immediately and went with him to the hospital. I was with him there for the next two hours until I judged that the crisis had passed." He passed his hand across his face again. "That crisis. There will be another one, I'm afraid."

He pushed back his chair and stood up.

"And now, Inspector, I'm going back to the hospital. I've told you everything I can." He picked up his overcoat and scarf and put them on. "I'm afraid it will be a miracle if Weston survives this, but I have to try."

Rodericks and Peele both stood up.

"I appreciate your help," Rodericks said, "the more so because I realize that all this must have been very hard on you personally. By the way, what happened to your car?"

Bannister looked blank for a moment. "My car? Oh, I see what you mean. I had my garage pick it up and deliver it at the hospital for me."

"Well, thank you again," Rodericks said. "You won't mind if Sergeant Peel types up the gist of what you have told us and gets you to sign it, will you? Of course, you'll have a chance to read it through first and correct us if any errors have crept in. And there is just one more thing. I understand Mrs. Weston is at the hospital with her husband?"

"That's right."

"I would like to talk to her sometime soon. Will she be spending the night there do you think?"

"I don't think so. I hope not. It depends on how her husband is when I get back. His condition is likely to remain critical for several days. If he lasts for a week he may have a chance of pulling through." He put on his gloves and took his car keys from his overcoat pocket. "To tell you the truth, I hadn't thought much about Lori. She'll have to sleep somewhere, and I don't suppose she'd care to come back here."

"Do you think that Mrs. Middleborough —"

"It might be the best thing," Bannister said. "The woman's a character but she has a heart of gold. And three bedrooms. Tell you what. I'll put it to Mrs. Weston and if she agrees, I'll bring her there myself. I'd rather not have her in the hospital overnight for her sake. There's nothing she can do. Can you fix it with Mrs. Middleborough?"

"I imagine so," Rodericks said. "But I'm afraid I'll really have to talk to Mrs. Weston tonight. So I'd rather you didn't give *her* any sedatives until I've done so." He stared at the doctor.

Bannister met his eye.

"Inspector Rodericks," he said very distinctly, "while I have every desire to assist the police in the performance of their duties, my duty is to my patients. I shall prescribe for them what and when I think fit. I hope I make myself clear."

"You do, sir," Rodericks replied evenly. "But I put it to you that it would look very strange if every member of the immediate family of the murdered woman was unavailable for questioning after the crime because of being under your care."

Dr. Bannister turned away angrily, then stopped and spoke over his shoulder.

"I shall certainly prescribe a sedative for Mrs. Weston tonight, but there is no reason why you should not interview her first if you think it important. You must, however, bear in mind that she has had two severe shocks today. If her husband's condition is unchanged, I'll bring her back here. You can talk to her and then she can spend the night at Mrs. Middleborough's."

Without waiting for an answer, Dr. Bannister stalked out of the room. A moment later the two policemen heard the front door slam behind him.

"A bit touchy, wasn't he?" said Sergeant Peele.

Rodericks smiled. "So would you be, if you had his job tonight. Just the same, when I have my coronary I hope I have somebody like him to look after me. Come on, Sergeant, let's go across the street and talk to Mrs. Middleborough."

"And perhaps to Miss Weston, sir?" asked Peele.

"Don't get zealous, Ted," Rodericks replied. "You heard the doctor — enough Nembutal to put her to sleep for twelve hours. It would be like talking to somebody who was under an anesthetic."

"I've heard that that's not always a waste of time," Peele said. "Not if you use the right anesthetic."

"You're missing your vocation with us," Rodericks told him. "The political police — that's where you ought to be."

5

MAPLE STREET was a tunnel of howling blackness under the night sky, but the sleet had stopped and the air was colder. Rodericks and Peele put their heads down against the savage wind and slithered across the icy roadway to Mrs. Middleborough's front door. As they went up the short walk a dog began to bark within the house.

Before Rodericks could find the doorbell, the door swung open six inches on a chain and a band of light spilled out across the black ice on the doorstep. A huge golden Labrador blocked the opening and pressed forward as though determined to jam himself immovably in the gap. He continued to bark ferociously, his head up and his body straining against the door. Above the dog a woman's face appeared, and a pair of bright black eyes looked at Sergeant Peele with a flicker of apprehension, then passed on to Inspector Rodericks.

The look of apprehension faded as the inspector was recognized for what he was, and there was the rattle of a chain. The door opened a little wider and the dog gathered himself together as though to spring.

"Back, Sam! Get back I say!"

A plump arm reached out and a beringed hand firmly grasped the Labrador's collar and pulled. The dog did not budge. He went on barking as loudly as before, although the effect of this was spoiled by the frantic wagging of his enormous tail. Mrs. Middleborough put her other hand on his collar and heaved.

"Get back, you brute! Go to the kitchen! Do you hear me?"

Reluctantly the Labrador backed away. He stopped barking and looked suddenly sad. Sergeant Peele patted him on the head as he entered and he had to lift his hand a good twelve inches to do so. Mrs. Middleborough slammed the door shut when the two detectives were in the hall. Then she turned her back on them, stamped her foot and pointed a commanding finger at Sam.

"Out!"

Sam's tail went down and he slunk away, looking dejected.

"Well," said Mrs. Middleborough, turning back to her visitors, "come in. I've been waiting for you."

With her hands on her hips, she stood to one side to let them precede her, a short stout woman in her early forties with elaborately waved black hair, an expensive looking black silk dress stretched tight across a formidable bosom and incongruously small, neat feet in black patent leather pumps. Roderick's first thought as he looked at her was that she seemed to have no neck, that her head was set directly on her shoulders like a toad's. His second thought was that there was an unmistakable gleam of intelligence in her eyes.

With his left hand he produced his identification card in its leather case and with his right hand he took off his hat. "I am Inspector Rodericks of the Ontario Provincial Police," he said politely, "and this is my assistant, Sergeant Peele."

Peele fumbled for his identification and displayed it. Mrs. Middleborough paid no attention.

"Go on in," she said, jerking her head in the direction they were to take.

Her living room was small and untidy. An open newspaper lay in sections on the floor beside an armchair. An empty cup and saucer and a plate covered with cake crumbs stood on a coffee table. A sealskin coat was draped over the back of another chair. The detectives found themselves backed up against the davenport.

"Sit down," said Mrs. Middleborough.

Rodericks moved a book that was lying face down on the davenport behind him and placed it on the coffee table, taking care not to lose the place. It was Jacqueline Susann's *Valley of the Dolls,* a work with which he was unfamiliar. He sat down. Sergeant Peele sat down beside him. The room was very warm. An electric fireplace scintillated in rose-colored flames a few feet from them.

Mrs. Middleborough plumped herself down in a chair across the room.

"I don't suppose you've caught him yet," she said.

"No, ma'am, not yet."

Rodericks was conscious that he sounded like the cop on *Dragnet,* and it irritated him. He found this surprising until he remembered that it was nearly ten o'clock and that he was hungry.

"And I don't suppose you will," Mrs. Middleborough said. "It's a shame the things we pay our taxes for."

Sergeant Peele took out his notebook and pencil, and Mrs. Middleborough eyed them belligerently.

"We'd like to ask you a few questions about what happened this evening," Rodericks said.

"Ann Weston's the one you should be talking to for that, but you can't. She's sound asleep, poor dear. And anyone who tries to wake her will have to do it over my dead body."

"I'll talk to Miss Weston in the morning," Rodericks said pleasantly. "What I'd like you to do is tell me your side of the story, if you would. You were in here, were you, when Miss Weston came to your door? What time would that have been?"

"I was in the kitchen eating my supper. And I don't know what time it was. Why should I? I've got better things to do than sit around watching the clock all day. It would have been around six-ten or six-fifteen, I suppose. I was in the kitchen having an early supper. Because of the storm. Normally on Tuesday nights I go to the Legion Hall to play bingo, but it was cancelled tonight. So I thought I'd have an early supper and watch TV."

She broke off and turned to glare at the Labrador who had poked his head beseechingly around the living room door.

"Back to the kitchen, Sam! Go on! Out you go!"

Sam drooped and retired, sure he was missing something.

"Yes, Mrs. Middleborough," Rodericks said gently. "You were saying?"

"The first I heard was when Sam started to bark. Then I knew there was somebody at the front door. Either that or a dog going by on the street. My doorbell is temporarily out of order, you see. Anyway, Sam was barking and then I heard this pounding on the door. I went to open it and Ann ran in, crying and sobbing so that I couldn't understand a word she was saying. She was half frozen too, for she had no hat or coat on. Nothing but that cocktail dress and it was soaked through. It'll be a wonder if she doesn't catch her death of cold, if nothing worse."

"I suppose her feet were wet too?"

"Wet? Wet? I should think they were wet. Up to her knees. And she was in her stocking feet. Didn't you hear about how she had to run out into her back garden?"

"Yes. Yes, I heard. And what did you do when you brought Miss Weston in?"

"I took her right out to the kitchen and made her sit down by the stove. I turned the oven on and opened the door. If she hadn't been in such a state, I would have tried to get her out of her wet clothes but I could see it was no use trying to do that until I found out what was wrong. It was quite a while before I could get any sense out of her."

"What was she saying during this time?"

"She wasn't saying anything anybody could understand. She was moaning and sobbing and rocking herself back and forth. Sometimes she said 'Aileen! Aileen!' And once she fainted dead away for a few seconds. When she came around she seemed calmer for a moment or two. That's when she told me her sister had been shot by a man who had forced his way into the house. As soon as she said that, I called Doctor Bannister. He lives just around the corner. I guess I was lucky to get hold of him like I did, and he said he'd go right around —"

Rodericks interrupted the flow. "Pardon me, Mrs. Middleborough, but did you say Miss Weston told you the man forced his way into the house? Are you sure that's what she said?"

"Why would I want to lie to you? Of course he forced his way in. Do you think those two girls would have let a strange man into the house after dark when they were all alone? Especially after the trouble they had had in the past week?"

"What trouble would that be?" Rodericks asked blandly.

"You don't know? My God, what are the police for, I'd like to know! You mean you haven't heard how those two girls were followed about by this sex fiend? Just waiting for his chance. Or about how he tried to break in through the pantry window only last night?"

"The kitchen window," Rodericks said. "Yes, I've heard something about it. What I was wondering was how you heard of it."

"Why, Lori told me," said Mrs. Middleborough. "Mrs. Weston, that is. She told me the whole story at noon today when she came over to borrow a 15-watt fuse. She said she was going to report it to the police. I told her it wouldn't do any good, that the police were fine at giving out parking tickets or at stopping you if you happen to go down an empty street at thirty-five miles an hour, but that they weren't any good for that sort of thing. And I was right, wasn't I? She did report it and it didn't do any good, did it? Aileen was killed just the same."

Rodericks regarded her benevolently. This seemed to put her out of countenance, and the aggressiveness of her manner noticeably abated.

"After you called the doctor, what did you do, Mrs. Middleborough?"

"Well, I came back to the kitchen — no, first I went and made sure the front door was locked, and then —"

"It had been locked when Miss Weston was pounding on it, had it? Otherwise she would have opened it and come in, I suppose?"

"No. No, as a matter of fact it wasn't locked. I don't know — I suppose she was too excited to get it open. And it sticks sometimes. The door sticks if you don't know how to open it."

"I see. It doesn't matter anyway. But after you locked the front door what did you do?"

"I locked the back door," said Mrs. Middleborough. For the first time she looked genuinely frightened. She put a pudgy hand up to her mouth and pulled nervously at her lips. A diamond-and-sapphire guard ring on her third finger glinted with white-and-blue fire.

"I'm not superstitious, but these things go in threes," she said. "Mark my words. There will be two more deaths before it's over. We may all be murdered in our beds."

"We must hope you're wrong. Now, Mrs. Middleborough, after you had locked both doors —?"

"After I locked the doors I came back to the kitchen and got out some brandy. I always keep some cooking brandy in the kitchen. I gave Ann a glass of it. I had to hold it for her. She was shaking so badly her teeth rattled on the rim of the glass. And I had a drink myself. Then I went and looked out the window and saw Dr. Bannister drive up. Oh yes, and I called the police."

"When did you call the police, Mrs. Middleborough? Not until after you saw Dr. Bannister arrive at the Westons?"

"No. I'm not sure. No, I think I called them before the

doctor came. Yes, I must have done." Mrs. Middleborough sounded flustered and a little defensive. "It was after I'd locked the doors and got the brandy, but before the doctor came."

"I see. And then what happened?"

"Well," said Mrs. Middleborough, "there wasn't anything more I could do for Ann, was there? She was all right in the kitchen by the stove."

"You stayed at the front window and watched?"

"Why not? Dr. Bannister had gone into that house all by himself, hadn't he? A brave man I think he is too. Why, the murderer might still have been in there! He might have been killed. But he never even hesitated. He ran right in, carrying his little black bag. The police were more cautious, I can tell you. I saw that Constable Holmsted looking all around before *he* went in. *And* he had his hand on his gun."

"What did you do after you saw the police come?"

Mrs. Middleborough looked a trifle uncomfortable, but only for an instant.

"Why, I went and got the doctor for poor Ann Weston, that's what I did. She was in a bad way by then. Shuddering and moaning there at the kitchen table, enough to break your heart. I went and got the doctor for her."

"And a very good thing you did, I'm sure," said Rodericks smoothly. "You and Dr. Bannister came back here together, I believe? And Corporal Moore?"

"That's right. He only came so he could pester the poor girl with questions though. It was downright cruel, it was. Luckily Dr. Bannister wasn't going to stand for any nonsense of that sort. He listened for a bit, then he said, 'You won't get anything worthwhile out of her in the condition she's in, Corporal,' he said. Quiet but firm. 'I'm going to give her a sedative,' he said, 'and the rest of your questions will have to wait until morning.' "

"And he gave her an injection then?"

"I suppose so. I went upstairs to get her room ready and put a hot water bottle in her bed. The next thing I knew Dr. Bannister was carrying her upstairs. I undressed her and got her into bed."

Rodericks stood up. My God, he thought, it is hot in here. I should have taken my overcoat off.

"Thank you very much, Mrs. Middleborough. I think that is all I need to ask you tonight. If any other questions occur to us, we will be back tomorrow. You will be asked to sign a statement later. And I'm afraid you will be required to give evidence at the inquest."

Mrs. Middleborough did not look at all disturbed by the prospect of this civic duty.

"And now, if you don't mind," Rodericks said, "I must ask you to take me up to Miss Weston's bedroom." He held up a hand as Mrs. Middleborough was about to burst into speech. "I shall not awaken her or disturb her in any way, but I must satisfy myself that she is all right. Would you please take me there at once?"

Mrs. Middleborough stared at him defiantly for a moment but her angry black eyes dropped before his cool gray ones. She turned without speaking and led the way upstairs. From the kitchen doorway Sam watched them with wistful eyes.

Ann Weston lay sound asleep in the middle of a large

double bed, her breathing deep and regular. When Rodericks switched on the bedside lamp the soft light fell across a pale face surmounted by a mass of tumbled chestnut hair. One bare arm lay outside the covers. The inspector took the girl's wrist and felt her pulse. Then he gently put a finger on her eyelid and lifted it. Mrs. Middleborough stirred in protest but Ann Weston did not move.

Rodericks turned away and switched out the lamp.

"Will you be sleeping nearby?" he asked. "So that you can hear her if she calls out in the night?"

"Just across the hall," said Mrs. Middleborough. "I'll leave both doors open. Not that I'll get much sleep, knowing that there's a homicidal maniac loose in the neighborhood."

"You will be quite safe, I assure you. My men will have your house under observation all night. But if you like, I'll have a constable actually stay here. Would that make you feel better?"

"No, it would not," said Mrs. Middleborough firmly. "Sam's better protection than any policeman I know. Thank you just the same."

"As you wish," Rodericks replied, and then suddenly remembered his promise to Bannister that he would try to arrange for Mrs. Weston to spend the night at her neighbor's. He suggested this a little diffidently and was surprised at the woman's reaction.

"Of course Lori can sleep here, Inspector. I intend to insist upon it." She sounded genuinely hurt that any other possibility could have been considered, but she spoiled the effect by adding in a self-righteous tone, "What are we here for if we can't help one another?"

When Rodericks descended the stairs he found Peele standing by the front door.

"The doctor's back," Peele said. "There's a lady with him. Probably Mrs. Weston."

Something in Peele's tone made Rodericks look at him questioningly. Peele opened the door, tipped his hat to Mrs. Middleborough and stepped out into the bitter wind. Rodericks followed him.

"This Mrs. Weston," Peele said. "I saw her going into the house."

"Yes," said Rodericks. "So you said."

"She's out of this world."

"Good-looking?"

"Good-looking? She's wonderful. I've never seen anything like it."

Rodericks glanced at Peele curiously. This was the first time he had heard the sergeant express any interest whatsoever in a woman since his wife had died.

"I gathered something of the sort from Corporal Moore," he said. "And from the photograph. It's strange."

"What's strange?"

"Oh, nothing really. It just strikes me as odd that of the three women in the Weston family our unknown killer murders the plain one. It's more often the other way around, you know."

6

Dr. Bannister and Lori Weston were sitting side by side on the settee in the back parlor. Lori wore a low-cut cocktail dress of sea-green tafetta that brought out the natural gold tints of her hair and matched her eyes. Looking at her, Rodericks could understand the effect she had obviously had on Corporal Moore and Sergeant Peele. He himself was not untouched by her beauty, although in the present circumstances it evoked in him a feeling that was almost akin to sadness. Perhaps, he thought, there was a fatality about Lori Weston.

He told himself abruptly that she was merely a woman who was involved in a murder case. Her astonishing loveliness was a fact like any other, something to be taken into consideration as having a possible relevance, but that was all. Rodericks did not even see how it could have any relevance, or at least any immediate relevance. It was his experience, though, that beautiful women often brought tension and conflict into the lives of those around them. Like a catalyst in a chemical process. No, that wasn't right either, for a catalyst caused a reaction in other substances, but was itself unchanged. Rodericks did not think that any woman could look like Lori Weston without it affecting her entire life.

These speculations took him through the introductions. Bannister was preparing to leave. He picked up his overcoat which was beside him on the settee, then put it down again and reached for his medical bag. He opened it and gave Lori a transparent plastic vial with two red capsules in it.

"Take one before going to bed," he said. "If you are still not asleep in half an hour, take the other."

Lori thanked him, taking his hand in both of hers and clinging to it for a moment. It was a natural gesture. When horror struck, friends were for clinging to. But Rodericks could sense that Peele was put out by it. For an instant he had almost bristled. Instinctive male jealousy would be a constant by-product of Lori Weston's beauty, the inspector thought.

When Bannister left, Rodericks and Peele drew up chairs facing Mrs. Weston. In the air near her there was a faint fragrance, so subtle that Peele was not consciously aware of it, but Rodericks, searching his memory, decided it was a perfume called *Je reviens*. Lori turned her gray-green eyes on the inspector.

"What do you want to know?"

Everything, Rodericks told her. Everything that she could tell them. They wanted to view the case through her eyes.

She began with her visit that afternoon to the police station, then went back to describe the incidents that had led up to it. She told of Aileen and Ann being followed home, of the second occasion when Ann alone was followed, and of the attempt the night before to break into the house through the kitchen window.

As she talked, Rodericks watched her face closely. She was pale and nervous but kept herself well under control. He guessed that she was at least as worried about her husband as she was grieving for Aileen. Again it was a natural reaction, but he sensed a reserve in her manner, as though there was something, some fact or some emotion, that she was concealing. After thirty years as a policeman he had an instinct for such things.

"You never saw this man yourself, Mrs. Weston?" he asked.

"No. On the night when both girls were followed home they told me that he was waiting outside the house. I looked but I saw nothing. He may still have been there, of course. The street is far too dark."

"And the second time?"

"I didn't go to the window that night."

"Why not?"

Lori looked away from the inspector. "Ann didn't tell me right away what the trouble was. I knew something was wrong, of course. She was white and trembling and out of breath. But by the time I got the story out of her—"

"She was reluctant to tell you?"

"Not exactly reluctant. I think she was afraid of making a fuss about nothing. And of her father getting to hear of it."

"Was there any danger of that?"

"He was in bed but we didn't know whether he was asleep or not. We kept our voices down."

"Did you — at the time, I mean, not now — did you think she might be making a fuss about nothing?"

Lori shook her head decisively. "No. Not the second time. You see, when Ann saw this man behind her, her first impulse had been to run. She didn't do that. Instead she stopped under the next streetlamp and looked back. And the man stopped too. That was really what frightened her — that and the fact that he was muffled up as though to conceal his identity."

Rodericks felt again, but more strongly this time, that she was keeping something back. He probed gently.

"Was there anything else about this second incident that was different from the first?"

Lori hesitated for a fraction of a second and Rodericks fixed her with his eyes. She colored and said, "It was only — perhaps I was wrong, but I thought that Ann was a good deal more disturbed than Aileen had been."

"Might that have been because Ann had seen the man twice? Because he seemed to be persistent?"

"Yes. Yes, that was probably it."

"Or was Ann more disturbed on the first occasion as well?"

Lori's hands fluttered in her lap and were immediately stilled.

"Was she?" The inspector's tone was quiet but persistent. Lori capitulated.

"Yes, she was. Much more upset than Aileen."

"Why do you think that was?"

Lori looked down at her hands. "I don't know," she said flatly.

"Could it have been because Ann recognized the man who was following them? That she knew who he was?"

Lori looked up at him resentfully.

"This is all guesswork," she said. "I've nothing to go on. You can't expect me —"

"Not quite guesswork, Mrs. Weston. An impression. That's a very different thing. What was your impression at the time?"

"I wondered if Ann had any idea who it was," Lori admitted. "No more than that. The chances are I was wrong."

Rodericks did not press her further. It would be settled once he was able to talk to Ann Weston. He thought it unlikely that any twenty-one-year-old girl would long be able to hide the truth from him. To his mind a more interesting question was whether he had discovered what it was that Mrs. Weston had been trying to conceal. He thought so, but he wasn't sure. There was still a shade of something other than grief and worry in her manner. Could it be fear? And if so, fear of what? Violence, murder and sudden death — or something else?

He took up the questioning again and listened carefully while she told him of going on from the police station to Molly Fitzpatrick's party.

"A Valentine party, Inspector. Today is Valentine's Day. The girls were going to go together at about six o'clock. Their fiancés were to meet them there."

"Their fiancés? I hadn't realized that Ann was engaged to be married. Corporal Moore told me that Aileen was."

"Both of them," said Lori. "They used to go out together as a foursome when the girls worked in London. Aileen became engaged last September and Ann at Christmastime."

She broke off and put a hand up to her mouth. "Oh dear!" she said, "Do you know, I don't suppose anyone has told Paul yet." She half rose, then sank back. "Isn't that awful? But I've had so much on my mind —"

"I'll look after it," Rodericks promised. "What's his name and address?"

"Paul Anstruthers, and he lives in London. Apartment 3, 131 Richmond Road. Fred lives there too. They share the apartment."

"Fred would be Miss Ann Weston's fiancé?"

"That's right. Fred Dunn. I don't know their telephone number, I'm afraid."

Rodericks got up with a murmured apology and went in search of Corporal Moore. He found him on the second floor going through Ann Weston's bedroom. He searched rapidly but neatly and very thoroughly, missing nothing. Rodericks watched him for a minute and was impressed. He wondered whether the police school gave a course on how to search a suspect's room. He had been in London so long that he was out of touch with what went on in the Toronto headquarters. If the school did not already have such a course on its curriculum, it could do worse than borrow Corporal Moore for a week or two.

"No sign of anything yet?"

Moore, who was taking a picture off the wall, grunted a negative, put the picture back where he had found it, stood back and straightened it with one finger.

"Not that I'd expect anything else," he said. "I've been through all the rooms on this floor and found nothing out of the ordinary. We won't, either, if you ask me, sir."

"Probably not, but go over everything anyway. In the

meantime you can put a call through for me." He gave the corporal Anstruthers' and Dunn's address, and added, "Get them both down here as soon as possible. By tomorrow morning at the latest. You can lay on transport if necessary. Tell them their presence is required to help the police in their investigation."

"Right, sir."

Moore took out a dresser drawer and set it carefully on the floor.

Rodericks left him to it and returned to the back parlor. Sergeant Peele was staring at Lori, seemingly tongue-tied, and Lori was gazing off into space as though he did not exist.

"Now, Mrs. Weston," Rodericks said. "Sorry to have left you like that. I won't keep you much longer and then Sergeant Peele will escort you over to Mrs. Middleborough's."

Lori looked at him. "That won't be necessary, thank you. I shall sleep here in my own room."

Rodericks knew from her tone that there would be no point in arguing with her. In any case, Corporal Moore had already searched her bedroom, so he had no objection.

"How long have you lived in this house, Mrs. Weston?" he asked.

"Four years and a bit. Five years next June to be exact. We moved in here immediately after our marriage. Before then my husband had a house on the south side of Farnham."

"Dr. Weston was a widower, I believe?"

"Yes, his first wife died nearly seven years ago, leaving him with Aileen and Ann, who were high school girls at that time." She bit her lip and her voice trembled. "We were happy here in those days. I had never belonged to a family before, you see. I was brought up in an orphanage. And now this! Poor Bob! It must have been awful for him! He was coming home tonight to change and then he was going on to the party."

"That's something I have wondered about," Rodericks said. "Your husband works in London, I understand? Did he drive back and forth? I haven't seen his car here."

"No, we sold his car after his heart attack last summer. He goes to the office by train. Usually he takes the 10:30 in the morning and comes back on the 6:05. As a rule I drive him to and from the station, but tonight, because of the party, he took a taxi." A spasm of grief twisted her face. "He was looking forward to it because he hasn't been out much since he got out of the hospital." She put a hand on Rodericks' arm as though to draw comfort from him. "If he dies now —"

"He may not," Rodericks said. Because he hated the banality of his own words, he added, "Dr. Bannister seemed to think there was some hope."

"George has been wonderful. I've known him for ten years but I never realized how devoted a doctor he was until tonight. If anyone can save him, he can." She drew a long, shuddering breath. "I'm sorry, Inspector. Did you want to ask me anything else?"

Rodericks would have liked to ask her about her relationship with the dead girl but he knew it was seldom worthwhile to put such a question so bluntly. Instead he said, "In a case of murder, Mrs. Weston, it is our unpleasant duty to ask personal questions that would, under any other circumstances, be impertinent and offensive. I hope you understand."

Lori Weston drew back as though he had struck her, her green eyes widening.

"Don't be alarmed, please. But I must ask about your family. Did your stepdaughters get on well together?"

Lori's hesitation was fractional but the inspector did not miss it. Then she said, very firmly, "They were devoted to one another."

"I see." He leaned forward and rested an elbow on his knee. "Mrs. Weston, please think carefully before you answer this question. Do you know of anyone — anyone at all — who could conceivably have wished to kill Aileen?"

"Most emphatically not. Both Aileen and Ann are — were — lovely persons. Aileen was very much in love and was looking forward to her marriage. Paul lectures at the university, and he has a sabbatical coming to him next term. They were going to spend it in France. Aileen was happy — happier than I've ever seen her."

Tears welled up in the lovely gray-green eyes but they did not fall. Lori Weston would not be a woman who cried easily or much, Rodericks thought.

"By the way, Mrs. Weston, there's one small point I'd like to clear up. You said that Mr. Anstruthers and Mr. Dunn were going to meet the girls at Mrs. Fitzpatrick's. I take it this plan was changed?"

"Yes, Paul telephoned Molly's before I arrived. He told her they had decided not to come because of the storm."

"That's strange," said Rodericks.

"What is?"

"That Mr. Anstruthers should telephone Mrs. Fitzpatrick to break the date for the evening. I should have thought he would have phoned here first and spoken to Aileen herself."

"He did," said Lori very quietly. "At about twenty past six. Nobody answered."

Rodericks deliberately kept his voice matter-of-fact. "That accounts for it. No, I don't think there's anything else tonight, is there, Sergeant?"

Peele shook his head. "Can't think of anything."

"Well then, thank you very much, Mrs. Weston. I'll probably have some other questions to ask you by tomorrow, but that will be all for now. I'm sorry to have to intrude upon you at a time like this."

Lori smiled faintly and rose to go. Rodericks stopped her before she got to the door.

"Oh, Mrs. Weston. There is just one thing that has occurred to me. Are any firearms kept in this house?"

Lori turned to face him. "Yes," she said. "My husband has a revolver. A war souvenir, I think. It's in his bureau drawer in our bedroom, together with a box of ammunition."

"Thank you, Mrs. Weston. Goodnight."

When Lori had left Rodericks turned to Peele. "You had better get on to headquarters, Ted. I want some mine-detectors down here right away."

Peele looked at him inquiringly.

"There's no revolver in the bedroom now," Rodericks explained. "And no box of ammunition. We won't know for sure until we check the registration records and the autopsy report, but it's a fairly good bet that the murder weapon came from the bureau drawer upstairs. We'll work on that assumption anyway. And that means that every inch of this house, the yard, the roadway and the streets for blocks around will have to be searched. Our murderer might easily have decided that a snow drift was the perfect hiding place."

"That means you think it was an inside job," Peele said.

"Not necessarily. But it means that it was probably done by someone who could get hold of Dr. Weston's revolver. I never did believe the theory that it was done by a stranger."

"Why not?" asked Peele. "I would have thought that after the previous incidents — but I see what you mean. You think it was done by someone Ann Weston knew."

"I've an open mind about that. But it was definitely done by someone Aileen Weston knew. Do you think she would have let a strange man into the house this afternoon? Taken him into the drawing room and talked to him in low tones? Mrs. Middleborough was quite right about that. No, Ted, this has all the marks of being a family affair. Now you go and arrange for those mine-detectors and then we'll try to get a bite to eat. Do you know it's eleven o'clock, and we haven't had any dinner?"

Peele looked at him sadly.

"I may not be a great detective," he said, "but I do know when I've missed eating."

He went in search of a telephone.

7

INSPECTOR RODERICKS sat behind the wheel of the police cruiser, letting the engine warm before he moved the car. The driver had been sent off an hour before to get his dinner and had not yet returned, a fact that privately disturbed Sergeant Peele. He hoped it did not mean that dinner would be hard to come by in Farnham. It was cold inside the car and the windshield was already frosting over with the breath of the two men. A current of icy air from the cold heater blew about their ankles. The time was ten minutes past eleven.

"Ted," said Rodericks, "I'm afraid there's one more little job we had better do before we eat. It shouldn't take long, but I want to talk to Mrs. Fitzpatrick tonight."

Peele sighed. "Sure," he said. He could feel his empty stomach grumbling. "We'll probably have to settle for hamburgers anyway. I shouldn't think there will be a restaurant open in this dump after ten o'clock."

It seemed to Peele that the old man was pushing it a bit far. The Fitzpatrick woman didn't strike him as being a vital witness. She could surely have waited until morning. Or at least until after dinner. So what if it was getting late? Another hour wouldn't make any difference. Of course, the inspector was always a hustler on a murder case. It was as though he took them personally. But this time he seemed more than usually obsessed with the value of time. Peele wondered why.

So, as a matter of fact, did Rodericks. He felt a sense of urgency that was almost oppressive, but when he examined this feeling he could find nothing that would logically account for it. Perhaps it was merely the frustration of not being able to interview the principal witness at once, but he did not really think so. He frowned in his effort to trace his uneasiness to its source. He always claimed that most of what passed for instinct was in fact experience that had been buried in the subconscious — knowledge by analogy, although by an analogy that had been incompletely drawn. If this was so, his memory failed him now, for he could think of nothing from the past that reminded him specifically of this case or that could account for his impulse to hurry. Although the green light was still glowing on the dashboard, he pulled the gear lever into drive and started off, his rear tires spinning in the wet snow.

Molly Fitzpatrick turned out to be a white-haired, gracious lady of fifty with a pleasant, white-haired husband who looked as though he might be a retired Colonel. They took the detectives into their living room, which was in impressive disorder. The furniture had been pushed back against the walls; empty glasses and dirty ashtrays littered every sidetable; cups and saucers, serving dishes and plates with crumpled paper napkins on them had been abandoned on any convenient flat surface. Sergeant Peele gazed hungrily at a half-empty platter of canapés sitting on a sideboard.

Mrs. Fitzpatrick's husband fingered his neat military moustache and sighed deeply as he looked about him.

"It was too late to warn them not to come," Molly Fitzpatrick said. "They began to arrive before Lori left. And, of course, they stayed on and on, talking about the murder and drinking gin. I'm sure everybody in Farnham knows about it by now."

Rodericks saw that it had indeed been a Valentine party. Hearts cut out of crimson paper decorated the walls and red crepe paper streamers hung down from the ceiling. A fat cardboard cupid with a bent bow beamed cherubically from above the mantel. There was a big bouquet of red roses beside the lamp on the hi-fi and bunches of forget-me-nots in twin vases at either end of the buffet. Molly Fitzpatrick had gone to a lot of work to make her party a success. Needless work, as it had turned out, for her guests would have remembered the evening as vividly if there had been no decorations at all.

"There doesn't seem to be any place to sit down," Mrs. Fitzpatrick said. "Would you like to come out to the kitchen? Although it's as bad there."

"We'll stand," said Rodericks. "And we won't take up much of your time. Just a few questions."

"But I don't know anything," Mrs. Fitzpatrick protested. "It's all horrible. Simply horrible!"

Rodericks agreed that it was horrible, then asked at what time Mrs. Weston had arrived.

"Lori? She got here about six-thirty. Actually, I had expected her sooner but she told me about stopping off on the way at the police station."

"And at what time did she leave here?"

"That nice Corporal Moore phoned her at about a quarter to seven. She left at once, of course, and went to the hospital. Is it true that Dr. Weston isn't expected to live?"

"I understand his condition is critical."

"How awful! And poor Aileen! Do you know, Inspector, I was talking to her just before she was killed? She sounded so bright and gay. I simply can't believe it!"

"You were talking to her in person?"

"Oh, not in person. Over the telephone. I phoned Lori to see if she would bring an extra ice bucket, but she had already left. Aileen said that she and Ann would be along in about half an hour."

"Can you remember what time this was, Mrs. Fitzpatrick?"

"About six o'clock. Perhaps a few minutes before. Two or three minutes before. Not more though. I know, because I was keeping a close watch on the time. My guests were due to start coming at six-thirty and of course I wasn't ready for them. I never am."

"What exactly did Aileen Weston say? Can you repeat the conversation as nearly as possible word for word?"

Mrs. Fitzpatrick looked doubtful. "Well, I don't know. It wasn't much. Not important, I mean. I asked if Lori was there and Aileen said no she was on her way over here, that she had left about ten minutes previously. She was surprised that she hadn't arrived yet, I think, but of course she didn't know about her visit to the police."

"Was anything else said?"

"Let me see," said Mrs. Fitzpatrick. "Aileen said, 'We'll be over as soon as Ann finishes dressing, and Dad will be along in about an hour.' Then I asked if she could possibly bring an ice bucket with her because I'd forgotten to get an extra one, and she said that Lori had already taken one in the car. She had too, bless her. That was exactly like Lori." Mrs. Fitzpatrick blinked rapidly to keep back her tears. "So thoughtful. And I hadn't even told her I would need it. Although I always do."

"Nothing else?" asked Rodericks. "That was all that was said?"

"That's all. It was a very short conversation. I was in a hurry, you see. I had a lot still to do."

Mr. Fitzpatrick spoke for the first time. "Have you any idea who it was?" he asked. "I mean, was it a robbery, or what? Someone who thought the house would be empty?"

"What makes you think that, sir?"

Mr. Fitzpatrick tugged at his moustache. "I don't know. A lot of people knew about our party here tonight. Knew that the Westons would be coming."

"It wasn't a robbery. Not as far as we know." Rodericks turned back to Mrs. Fitzpatrick. "This may seem a silly question, but are you absolutely sure that it *was* Aileen Weston you were talking to?"

"Of course, I'm sure. It was her voice. I'd know it anywhere."

"Thank you, Mrs. Fitzpatrick. Oh, there is one other thing. I believe Mr. Anstruthers called here to say that he and Mr. Dunn couldn't get to the party because of the storm. Is that right?"

"That's right. Paul called at about half past six — just before Lori came. He said he had phoned the Westons' to try and get Aileen but that there wasn't any answer." Molly Fitzpatrick put a well-manicured hand up to her mouth and gave a little gasp. "I suppose that was *when*," she said. "I mean, if there wasn't any answer at the Westons' it must have happened by then. *Or have been happening*." She looked sick, and she was still looking sick a few moments later when Rodericks and Peele took their leave.

Out in the car again, Rodericks said, "Farnham will bar its doors tonight."

Sergeant Peele cared little for the fear that might stalk the streets of Farnham or for the burghers who would bar their doors. Another thought was uppermost in his mind.

"That lets Mrs. Weston out," he said with obvious satisfaction. "She has the perfect alibi. She can actually prove she was at the police station talking to Moore at the time the murder was committed."

Rodericks made no reply. It occurred to his suspicious mind that Mrs. Weston's alibi was almost too perfect. Yet if Aileen had been alive at six o'clock and dead at twenty past, it was obviously impossible for her stepmother to have been the killer. Of course, there were other possibilities . . . He told himself that these suspicions were probably nonsense, his old habit of making extra work for himself. He started the car and pulled away from the snow drift that covered the curb.

"There's a hotel I noticed on Main Street on the way in," he said. "Let's see if they can find us anything to eat and put us up for the night. We've done all we can for now."

Bagshott's Hotel was nothing much to look at from the outside — a three-story frame building with a hideous stucco front. Inside, the lobby was small and dark and smelled equally of age and stale beer; there were a few leather armchairs stuffed with horsehair; and behind a glass-topped desk in a corner a very old man in spectacles read a last year's copy of *Life*. Nevertheless, ten minutes after they had entered the place, Rodericks and Peele were seated at a corner table in a cosy dining room, drinking beer out of pewter tankards and eating a delicious meal of cold roast beef sliced very thin, pickles, green salad and homemade bread which they cut from a loaf on the table.

"A bit better than hamburgers, Ted," Rodericks said as he beckoned a waiter and ordered another tankard of beer. "Some of these old places are surprisingly good still. Not many, but some."

"A good job we got rooms when we did. Farnham will be swarming with reporters by tomorrow morning. I imagine only the storm has kept them away so far." Peele pushed his empty plate from him and put his elbows on the table. "Well, sir, what do you make of it?"

Rodericks took another pull at his tankard and wiped his mouth with his napkin. "I don't know yet. But I'm beginning to get some very peculiar ideas."

"Such as?"

"Such as Mrs. Weston's story of the man who was molesting her stepdaughters. For the moment I pass over the fact that so far we have only Mrs. Weston's word for any of it. No doubt Ann Weston will confirm it all in the morning. But doesn't it strike you that this molester was quite remarkably ineffectual?"

"That's common enough," Peele said. "Queers are often

like that. Nervous and timid. You find the same thing with exhibitionists and the guys that get their kicks stealing bits of clothing."

"Perhaps. But then someone — presumably the same man — attempts to break into the Weston house. And how does he do it? He walks through about three feet of snow to the kitchen window, attacks the window frame with a chisel for no good reason that I can see, breaks a pane as loudly as he can and then runs off. What do you think of that? Pretty stupid, isn't it?"

"Unfortunately, he wasn't so stupid when it came to concealing his identity."

"Quite so," said the inspector.

"We can't make anything out of his footprints," Peele said. "They were pretty well washed out by the sleet."

"No. But the other set of footprints is more interesting."

"Ann Weston's? They prove she did what she said she did."

"They prove she went into the garden sometime, yes. Oh, at about six or six-fifteen, I'll grant you that. The amount of erosion would be about right, I suppose. Some expert might even be able to testify to the time by comparing our photographs with the amount of precipitation. Although I'm always damned suspicious of that kind of calculation."

"So are juries," said Peele.

"They've got more sense than the experts, that's why. And it's also why we have juries. But what I meant was something else. Did you notice the spacing of Ann Weston's footprints? She went out to the back of the garden slowly, creeping along the wall, for those footprints are close together and relatively shallow. Her footprints coming back to the house were farther apart and deeper — only toeprints really. That is to say, she was running on her return journey."

Sergeant Peele thought about this and as he did so his face became longer and sadder. At last he said, "What about Mrs. Middleborough's story that the murderer forced his way in?"

"What she actually said was that Ann Weston told her the murderer had forced his way in."

"Sure," said Peele. "I know."

"It's not Corporal Moore's recollection of what was said, nor Dr. Bannister's."

"She might have told different stories. One to Mrs. Middleborough when she came running over there right after the murder and another to Moore and the doctor when she had had a chance to think it over and remember it better."

"Yes," said Rodericks, and there was a certain grimness in his tone. "Yes, she might." He gave a little shrug. "On the other hand, Mrs. Middleborough was wrong about which window was broken. She said the pantry, not the kitchen. She may be habitually inaccurate. Anyway let's leave it until tomorrow when we can talk to Ann Weston herself."

"I'll tell you what would be nice though," Peele said. "It would be nice to get our hands on the murder weapon. This kind of speculation is all very well, but juries like to see things with their own eyes. Like a revolver with a big red tag on it saying 'Exhibit A.' "

Before the inspector could answer a shadow fell across their table and both men looked up to see the stumpy figure of Dr. McCabe standing beside them. He reached out, took hold of a chair and sat down.

"That beer you're drinking?" he asked. "I'll have some. Hey, waiter!"

He said nothing more until the waiter returned with three full tankards. Then he said "Mud in your eye," took a long swallow, and reached in his overcoat pocket for a notebook. He flipped through the pages quickly, found what he wanted and put the notebook on the table in front of him.

"All right," he said. "I can give you the gist of it now. You wouldn't understand the autopsy report anyway. It's always full of goddamn Latin." He took another drink and added, "You've got a murder on your hands."

Rodericks beamed at him, as a teacher might beam at a not-very-bright pupil who had unexpectedly supplied the correct answer to a question.

"A nasty goddamn murder," McCabe repeated. "The body was that of a young woman, twenty-three to twenty-six years old. A virgin, in case it means anything to you. Six bullets were fired. I recovered them all, by the way, so there won't be any goddamn argument about that. Two bullets passed through the lower jaw. One inflicted a superficial scalp wound above the left temple. Three bullets were fired at point-blank range into the heart. Any one of those three would have caused death instantly. No way of knowing which one did. But I can tell you this — the three wounds in the heart were inflicted after the three wounds in the head. Some little time after."

"Of course I believe you," Rodericks said. "Just tell me how you know."

"Blood," said McCabe. "There was a lot of blood. More

than you'd think. There was a pool of blood under the body, down by the waist and hips. A pool about eighteen inches long and six inches wide. I found a bullet in that pool of blood. A bullet with a chip of tooth still sticking to it."

"This blood came from the head wounds, I take it?"

"Goddamn right it did. From the scalp wound mostly. The two jaw wounds didn't bleed much, and there was practically no external bleeding from the breast wounds. Those bullets didn't exit. They were right there in the heart."

"And, of course, the scalp wound would stop bleeding soon after death, wouldn't it?"

"Right," said McCabe. "You don't need me. You can work the rest of it out for yourself." He finished his beer and made as though to get up.

"Not so fast," said the inspector. "Why deduce when we can be told? Finish your story."

McCabe settled back in his chair. "We can measure the rate of bleeding pretty accurately in this case. I won't go into details here, but this is what happened. The girl was shot three times in the head. She fell to the floor — off her chair, I would guess — those three wounds are all slanting slightly downward. Right? She falls to the floor, bleeding and almost certainly unconscious. Whoever fired the shots looks at the mess he's made and figures she's dead. He goes away — oh, for maybe ten minutes, maybe a little less, there was quite a lot of blood, as I said — then he comes back and finds she's not dead after all. She has moved. Maybe she's even trying to sit up. So he puts the gun right up against her and gives her the other three wounds. I hope you catch the goddamn son-of-a-bitch."

He put his hand in his overcoat pocket and with something of a flourish produced two small cardboard boxes. He opened both of them and held them under the inspector's nose. Inside one, lying on cotton wool, were five slightly flattened lead bullets. The other box contained only one bullet and a small piece of cardboard with a microscopic sliver of tooth fixed to it. "You're looking for a .32 caliber revolver," McCabe said. "Probably a pretty old pattern, if the ammunition's anything to go by. Have you found it yet?"

"Not yet," said Rodericks. "We're still looking."

"This ammunition has probably been lying around for years. Most .32 caliber today is nickel plated."

"And smokeless," said Rodericks. When McCabe cocked an eyebrow at him, he explained. "Both the doctor and Corporal Moore mentioned that they smelled cordite. I don't know that it helps much. We seem to have narrowed the time of death down to about twenty minutes without it."

"Not from the medical evidence you haven't," said McCabe. "Or not from my medical evidence. The nearest I can come to it is between four and seven o'clock. Just as I said, you didn't need me. I had that goddamn drive for nothing."

"You're indispensable, Mac. By the way, who did you get to help you?"

"A young fellow called Saunders. We did the autopsy at the local hospital. Not half bad either. These young doctors don't know how lucky they are. When I was Saunders' age, as often as not I did my autopsies on a kitchen table."

"By the light of an oil lantern, I'm sure."

McCabe glowered at the inspector, but before he could retort, Sergeant Peele, who had been sitting with an abstracted look on his face, interrupted.

"How can you know that she moved?" he asked. "Couldn't he have shot her again where she was lying?"

McCabe stood up. "Ask your boss that one, son," he said. "Good night all."

Sergeant Peele stared resentfully after the little pathologist. "All right. I'm stupid. No, don't tell me. I can work it out myself." He sat frowning for a minute, then said, "Easy isn't it? The pool of blood under the hips, and the bullet with a piece of tooth on it. She had to have moved. But she didn't have to do it herself, did she? Somebody could have moved her."

"They could," Rodericks agreed, "but I expect McCabe's right. It has the ring of truth, I'm afraid." He sat quite still for about two minutes, his face expressionless, then he stood up.

"Excuse me, Ted. I've a couple of phone calls to make. Be right back." Ten minutes later he returned and sat down. "Well, that's fixed," he said.

Peele raised an eyebrow at him.

"There'll be a police matron out within an hour to sit beside Miss Weston's bed for the rest of the night. In the meantime, I've got a constable outside her room in the hall."

"You think the wrong girl was killed then? That the murderer may try again?" Peele sounded excited.

Inspector Rodericks shook his head. "It's possible. But that's not what I'm worried about. I wish it were."

"What is it then? If she's not in any danger, why the guard?"

"I didn't say she wasn't in any danger," said Rodericks sadly. He was thinking of his own daughter, who would now be safely at home studying the history of Anglo-Saxon literature for her comprehensives next month. Ann Weston was about the same age. And he remembered another girl — someone who had been in far less serious trouble than Ann Weston might conceivably be in — but who had nevertheless slashed both her wrists with a razor blade and bled quietly to death in her own bathroom before the police realized that something was wrong and broke down the door. The memory weighed on his heart even now, although it had happened all those years ago.

"It's not settled yet, of course," he said, "but a case seems to be building up." When Peele still looked blank, Rodericks added, "Has it never occurred to you, Ted, that we've only got Ann Weston's word for it that anyone came to the door this afternoon?"

8

RODERICKS SLEPT THAT NIGHT on a brass bedstead in a shabby room with sepia wallpaper. He had been too tired to read a line of Tolkien or to care about his surroundings, but in the morning he looked about him almost with awe. Apart from the floral design on the wallpaper, there was absolutely nothing in the room that was not severely utilitarian. Light was provided by a single unshaded bulb in the ceiling, and even the Gideon Bible was used as a doorstop to keep the clothes closet shut. He had to go down the hall to the communal bathroom to shave. It disturbed his thrifty soul to reflect that the taxpayers of Ontario were being charged twelve dollars a night for this accommodation.

However, breakfast more than compensated for the inadequacies of the bedroom. He and Peele were first presented with full tumblers of orange juice; then a platter appeared, heaped high with fried bacon, sausages, slices of fried ham, grilled kidneys and four fried eggs; a small mountain of hot buttered toast was placed in front of them; and the waiter plugged in a battered nickel coffee pot which held eight cups of real coffee. With a sort of hypnotic satisfaction Rodericks watched the slow bubbling of the aromatic brown liquid against the glass top of the percolator. It cost him an effort of will to turn away and concentrate on what Sergeant Peele was saying.

"— it looks to me as though we're on to something. I don't suppose Ann Weston would be used to firearms. She had probably never handled a revolver before."

"Before?" said Rodericks. "Well, if she murdered her sister with her father's revolver, I expect you're right. But Ted, that's not at all the same thing as saying that since she had never handled a revolver before she therefore murdered her sister."

"How's that again?"

"The proposition isn't reversible. 'If P then Q' is not the same as 'if Q then P.' I don't suppose that one person in a hundred in the population has ever fired a pistol, and not one in a thousand is reasonably expert at it. We've still quite a way to go before we're ready to make an arrest. For one thing there isn't the slightest shadow of a motive so far."

"We don't need one," said Peele.

"It helps. When you hear that the crown doesn't have to prove motive you mustn't start believing that it applies to policemen. The crown will certainly expect *us* to prove motive. Unless the case is otherwise absolutely open and shut."

"Which this one isn't." Peele ate steadily for a minute or two before he spoke again. "I couldn't get to sleep last night," he said, "so I got up and typed out the statements."

"Good," said Rodericks. "Send a copy off to the crown attorney this morning. Moore will see to it for you. It's best to keep our masters informed of what we're doing."

Peele was not distracted. He nodded an acknowledgement

of the instruction and said, "After I finished the typing I began thinking."

Rodericks looked politely interested.

"First, either Ann Weston is telling the truth or she isn't."

"That would seem to be eminently logical."

"If she isn't, she probably did it herself."

"That's quite a leap," Rodericks said, "but it would certainly bear looking into."

"If she is telling the truth, there are two possibilities. First, it was done by a psycho. Whom we may or may not find. And who may or may not kill again. Second, it was done by somebody Aileen Weston knew, somebody she would let into the house, somebody who knew about the revolver in the bedroom upstairs."

"Somebody," amended Rodericks, "who had already removed the revolver from the bedroom upstairs. The murderer had the weapon with him when he came into the house."

"That's right." Peele thought about this for a moment or two. "Anyway, what I say is this — so far the most likely bet is that Ann Weston is lying. So we haven't any motive. But we do have some other things against her, and that's more than we have against anybody else."

"We've a lot of work to do yet," said Rodericks.

"I don't know what more we can do. Grill Ann Weston, of course. But what else?"

"Not 'grill,' Ted. You sound as though you carried a piece of rubber hose in your pocket. We will question Ann Weston, certainly."

"All right. And if she sticks to her story what do we do then?"

Rodericks poured himself a third cup of coffee. "We talk to people."

"We already have."

"We do it again. In a case like this, Ted, where there are not very many material clues and no obvious suspect, all we can do is talk to people. Over and over again. We get the same story half a dozen times. Only it's never exactly the same story."

"I don't follow you."

"Well," said Rodericks, "it's rather like those four books by Lawrence Durell, which are really all the same book. He retells the identical plot each time, but in each case it's seen through the eyes of a different person. A very interesting technique, although to my mind he spoils it by talking too much about bruise-colored clouds on oyster-colored skies."

Peele, who had never read the *Alexandria Quartet,* looked baffled.

"What's important," Rodericks explained, "is the differences."

"You mean we catch someone lying?"

"Eventually, of course. But to start with it's enough if something looks queer, out of place. And," he added thoughtfully, "we already have an instance or two of that." He took his pipe out of his pocket and saw that it was already filled from the night before. He lit it carefully. "And now," he said, "if you're sure you've had enough to eat, let's get on with it."

In the lobby they were stopped by three reporters, but Rodericks fobbed them off with a short factual statement about the murder.

"The inquest will be held in the next day or two. Final arrangements haven't been made yet. That's all I can tell you now. No, I wouldn't say that an arrest is imminent. You can say we're following up several interesting leads."

The newspapermen were not happy about it but they knew Rodericks and were aware that he never gave anything away to the press unless publicity would help him break a case. They grumbled as they followed him out to the car, snapped a few pictures of him and Peele as they were getting into the back seat and waved a cheery good-bye.

This morning there were five police cars parked on Maple Street in the vicinity of the Weston house. Two of them were the vehicles from London that had brought down the eight constables who had been working with mine-detectors most of the night. Once again Corporal Moore was waiting on the verandah. Although it was only eight o'clock, he had been on the job for more than an hour and he had a number of items to report.

In the first place, the search for the murder weapon had proved fruitless. The Weston house had been gone over inch by inch; so had Mrs. Middleborough's, to that lady's considerable indignation; the garden, front lawn and the roadway on both sides of the house had been combed with mine detectors, but no trace of the revolver had been found.

The inspector, who remembered Lizzie Borden's axe, was not satisfied and ordered the whole process to be repeated once again. Corporal Moore, who had anticipated exactly this command, merely said 'Yes, sir,' and continued with his report.

"I checked our records at the station. Dr. Weston had a

.32 caliber Smith and Wesson six-shot revolver registered in his name. A house permit only; he couldn't carry it with him."

"Somebody has been breaking the law then," said Rodericks facetiously.

Moore did not smile. "It's a common enough gun, sir," he said.

"Have you anything else?"

It seemed that in the basement of the Weston home a chisel had been found — Corporal Moore displayed it as he spoke — and the chisel blade fitted the marks on the frame of the kitchen window. There were also faint traces of white paint along the chisel's cutting edge which matched the paint of the windowsill. None of this was conclusive, for the tool was a standard size and the entire house was trimmed with the same white paint, but Rodericks, who believed that it was good policy to keep the experts busy, ordered the chisel sent to the forensic laboratory in London for tests.

"Now, sir, there's something else," Moore said. "Miss Weston has moved back to her own room in this house. Dr. Bannister was against it, but she said that if her stepmother could stay here so could she. And she won't let the police matron in, sir. Mrs. Weston and Dr. Bannister both supported her in that and there was a bit of a row, I'm afraid. They claim that it's their house and that unless Miss Weston is under arrest she doesn't have to have policewomen in her bedroom."

"Did you talk to Miss Weston yourself, Corporal?"

"No, sir, I had no chance to. But I talked to Mrs. Weston and to Dr. Bannister."

"Very well. Miss Weston, of course, is within her rights, but I'll speak to her myself. Is the matron still here?"

"She'll be waiting at the station by now, I expect, sir. I told her she might as well go and get herself some breakfast."

Rodericks pondered for a moment. "Send her back to London," he said at last. He told himself that, if when he interviewed Ann Weston he believed her to be lying, he would take no chances. He would arrest her first and dig out the evidence afterwards.

"One other thing, sir," Moore said. "There's another resident, as you might say. That young fellow Dunn you wanted down here. He showed up half an hour ago and moved into the spare bedroom. Mrs. Weston said it was all right, so there was nothing I could do about it. He claims he's going to marry Miss Weston."

"Yes, I know, Corporal. Perhaps it's just as well. We'll have him under our hand if we want him. Did Dunn arrive in Farnham by himself, do you know?"

"No, sir. He came with Mr. Anstruthers, the dead woman's fiancé. But he's put up at Bagshott's Hotel, he told me. He and Dunn are both in the back parlor now, waiting for you."

The two young men who were waiting in the back parlor to interview the police were nervous. Rodericks also had the impression that they had been quietly quarreling immediately before he entered. If so, they stopped when they heard him coming, but they turned to face him with the air of suppressed anger that married couples sometimes display when they have been interrupted in a domestic squabble.

Paul Anstruthers was a heavy-set, full-faced man of about

twenty-five, strikingly handsome in his way, with tightly curling brown hair and bright amber eyes. He looked like some youthful Roman emperor — Nero, perhaps, or Commodus, in the early years before dissipation and power had completely corrupted them. Rodericks did not get the impression that he was grief-stricken over the violent death of his fiancée. Fred Dunn looked like a monkey on a stick — a small, wizened, very intelligent monkey who wore glasses and had acquired a certain charm of manner. Remembering the tall girl in the photograph, Rodericks thought that he seemed the last person in the world to be engaged to Ann Weston. The inspector had long ago given up trying to understand what made a particular man attractive to a particular woman, although he believed he knew as much as the next about the converse situation. All the same, given the two in front of him and the two girls in the photograph, he would have guessed that Anstruthers might possibly have been engaged to Ann and that Aileen, tired perhaps of waiting and feeling spinsterhood creeping up on her, might have settled for Dunn.

"This must be a very sad and painful experience for you, Mr. Anstruthers," Rodericks began, "and I certainly do not wish to prolong or aggravate it in any way."

Paul Anstruthers looked solemn and nodded his massive head.

"There are a few points that must be cleared up, though." The inspector turned to Fred Dunn. "Mr. Dunn, I understand that you are now staying in this house?"

Dunn took off his glasses and rubbed them nervously against his coat sleeve. "That's right, Inspector. Ann needs me around for a day or two."

"Of course. That's very understandable. May I ask if you are planning to be married soon?"

"Fred," said Anstruthers, turning to his monkey-faced friend, "what do you suppose all this has to do with Aileen's murder?" His manner of speaking sounded the least bit affected, for his tone was higher than normal and his enunciation very precise.

Dunn ignored him. "No date has been set for the wedding, Inspector," he said, "but I hope it will be soon. The sooner the better really. Ann should get right away from all this."

"She may not want to leave, Fred, while her father is so ill." Anstruthers was bland but Rodericks thought that this was somehow a continuation of their interrupted quarrel. "It's up to you, of course — and Ann —"

Before Dunn could reply, Rodericks broke in, "Yes. Well, all I actually want from you two gentlemen is a little background information. I understand that you are lecturers at the university?"

"Assistant professors, actually," said Anstruthers.

Rodericks smiled at him. "I beg your pardon, sir." The respect in his tone was the slightest bit exaggerated. "I'm afraid I wouldn't know the difference. I never had the opportunity to go to a university myself. Now if you could tell me how long you have known the Weston girls, when you became engaged to them, and whether either of you can think of anyone, however unlikely, who might wish to see Miss Aileen Weston dead?"

For a moment Rodericks thought that Paul Anstruthers was going to speak. He lifted his big head a fraction of an inch and a muscle near the corner of his mouth twitched but his amber eyes remained as blank as a cat's. The moment passed and Dunn was the one who replied for both of them.

"We met Ann and Aileen last summer. Pretty soon we were all going out together as a foursome. Then Paul became engaged to Aileen."

Rodericks fancied he could detect some strong, suppressed emotion in the ugly little man. Bitterness? Jealousy? Regret for golden friendship gone?

Dunn went on, "This Christmas Ann and I decided to marry. As far as your second question is concerned, the answer is no. We have no idea in the world who could have murdered Aileen. It's incredible. Surely it must be the work of a maniac?"

Rodericks did not seem to have heard the question. "You say you met the girls for the first time last summer. I wonder if you would be a little more definite than that. Just when last summer?"

Dunn screwed up his face and narrowed his eyes in thought. "August," he said. "About the middle of August. It was on a weekend at the lake." He turned to Anstruthers. "About the eighteenth?" he asked. Anstruthers nodded.

Rodericks looked into the blank amber eyes and smiled. "And you became engaged in September, I think you said, Mr. Anstruthers?"

"I didn't say. But that is correct. Near the end of September. Presumably you have your reasons for this line of questioning, Inspector — I have had very little experience with policemen myself — but what has any of this to do with finding a murderer? That *is* your aim, I take it?"

Rodericks twinkled at him as though they shared some excellent private jest, and went on as though nothing untoward had been said. "And you agree with Mr. Dunn that no one would profit from Miss Aileen Weston's death?"

"Well," said Anstruthers with a sidelong glance at Dunn, "I certainly agree that we know of no one who would wish to murder Aileen. As Fred says, it must be the work of a maniac."

The inspector spoke sharply. "This is a case of murder, Mr. Anstruthers. Equivocation, from whatever motive, is out of place and could be dangerous. Am I to understand that, although you can think of no one who would wish Miss Weston dead, you *do* know of someone who would profit from her death?"

Anstruthers flushed and his voice went up half an octave. "I resent your tone, Inspector. I resent it very much. They told me you were in charge of homicide in the London bureau. If so, surely you know that there is almost always someone who profits from any death. Fortunately though, that is not at all the same thing as murder or even the desire for death. Please don't try to put words into my mouth."

Rodericks looked at him thoughtfully. There was, all at once, something remarkably feminine about this burly young man with a face that might have been copied from a Roman coin. He paid no attention to the protest, but merely asked, "Do you know of anyone who profits from Miss Aileen Weston's death?"

Anstruthers shrugged. "No. I don't know. I believe she had money of her own which she inherited from her mother, but I never inquired about the details. I'm not a fortune-hunter, Inspector." He looked at Rodericks, his eyes suddenly very shrewd. "Did she leave a will?"

"A good point, sir," said Rodericks, as though it had not

previously occurred to him. "We'll have to check that, won't we?"

"Not that it will prove anything, of course." There was a hint of malice in Dunn's voice. "If Aileen left a will, Paul here will probably inherit, I should think. And any idea that —"

He broke off, leaving his unfinished sentence hanging in the air like a puff of some invisible but lethal gas.

The inspector allowed the silence to become noticeable, then asked, "What time was it when you telephoned here yesterday afternoon, Mr. Anstruthers?"

"About twenty past six," Anstruthers replied. "There was no answer. I let the phone ring five or six times, then called Mrs. Fitzpatrick and told her Fred and I wouldn't be able to make it."

"Was Mr. Dunn with you at the time?"

"Do you mean while I was telephoning? Yes, as a matter of fact he was. We were in the apartment together. When we decided that the driving was too bad for us to risk it, I got on the phone to let the girls know."

"And what did you do after that?"

"Fred and I had dinner together," Anstruthers said. "Then Fred went to a movie and I went back to the apartment. We were wakened by one of your policemen, in the early hours of this morning, at about one o'clock, and told the news of Aileen's murder. We drove down together after breakfast."

"Thank you," said Rodericks, "I think that's everything for the time being. You will be asked to read over and sign the statements which Sergeant Peele will prepare. You will both be in Farnham for the next few days, I take it?"

"Do you mean," asked Anstruthers, "that we're not allowed to leave?"

Rodericks looked shocked. "Certainly not, sir. Whatever gave you that idea? Of course, you may be required to give evidence at the inquest, but as long as I know where I can get hold of both of you, you are perfectly free to come and go as you please."

When Dunn and Anstruthers had departed, Rodericks looked at Peele and raised an eyebrow.

"That's the queerest damn set-up I've ever seen," said Peele. "And I do mean queer. Who would have thought that those two lover boys would have turned up in the role of fiancés?"

"Yes," said Rodericks absently. "Yes, I expect you're right. That was certainly my impression."

He was by no means free from prejudice and he had taken an instinctive dislike to the two young academics. This was partly because he was sufficiently old-fashioned to feel an unenlightened distaste for any suggestion of sexual perversion, but he was a just man and he reminded himself that there might be other, less creditable reasons. Was there still a little, lingering bitterness over the fact that he had been unable to attend college during the depression of the thirties? He examined the possibility coldly and decided in his own favor. Apart from anything else, Anstruthers and Dunn had more brains than judgment and more arrogance than common sense. He told himself sourly that they were probably vociferous ideological pacifists, the kind who signed petitions and marched in the less dangerous demonstrations — not civil rights marches in the deep South but sidewalk parades in front of the United States Consulate between teatime and dinner. Two eminently kickable young men. The deliberate lapse from charity left him feeling better.

He walked over to the baby grand piano and stared down at the family photograph in its silver frame, but his mind was still on the unlikely fiancés of the two sisters. "Rosencrantz and Guildenstern," he said half to himself, "the obliging friends."

Sergeant Peele had read *Hamlet* in his time but had not thought much about it. As a rule, he saw no reason to respond to his superior's literary allusions. He followed this rule now, and after a moment Rodericks continued.

"Here is a point to consider. What was it that made the Weston girls become engaged to those two gentlemen? Ann at least is very attractive. Were they desperate to leave home? Or what?"

"Mrs. Weston told us that Aileen was crazy about Anstruthers," Peele reminded him. "No accounting for tastes, of course."

"Yes. I remember. No one has said that Ann is crazy about Mr. Fred Dunn though. In fact, I thought there was a certain reserve on that subject."

"He's living here."

Rodericks sighed. "So he is. I must ask Miss Weston why."

Just then Dr. Bannister appeared in the doorway and Rodericks strode over to greet him.

"Good morning, Doctor. How are the patients today?"

Bannister's face had lost much of its boyish charm. He looked exhausted and irritable, as though he had had little sleep. "Dr. Weston spent a bad night," he said, "but he's resting somewhat easier now. It's going to be touch and go."

"Of course I'm sorry to hear it, Doctor, but I'm afraid I was really more interested in Miss Ann Weston. When can I expect her down?"

"You can't," said Bannister bluntly. "Ann's in no fit shape to be interrogated. I'm sorry, but as her physician I can't allow it."

When he replied, Rodericks' voice was so soft that Sergeant Peele looked up with quick alarm. He knew from experience that that gentle tone boded trouble for someone.

"You may be surprised to learn, Doctor, that the police still have certain rights in this country, more or less commensurate with their duties. Now it is my clear duty to interrogate Miss Ann Weston without any more delay and I intend to do so. You would be well advised not to hinder me further."

"Further?" said Dr. Bannister angrily. "What the devil do you mean by 'further'? If you are suggesting that quietening a dangerously hysterical woman before she went into a state of shock is hindering the police, you can go to hell. I'm telling you right now that Ann Weston is in no fit condition to be badgered with a lot of questions. It might do her permanent, irreparable damage —"

Rodericks broke in, but he still spoke gently. "And I tell you, Doctor, that if Miss Weston is not downstairs prepared to talk to me within the next half hour, I shall arrest her as a material witness."

"This is outrageous!" Bannister declared, white with rage. "Another twenty-four hours of rest will make all the difference to Ann and it cannot conceivably make any difference to your investigation."

A clear voice from behind the two men interrupted the quarrel.

"What seems to be the trouble?" Lori Weston asked. "George, why on earth are you making so much noise? Ann's trying to sleep. I could hear you shouting up in my room."

This unexpected attack from the rear left Bannister momentarily speechless.

Mrs. Weston was wearing a plain black housecoat which buttoned up to the throat. It emphasized the rich gold tints of her hair. Sergeant Peele thought that her hair looked almost like a halo as it caught the single ray of morning sunlight that came in through a gap in the drapes across the bay window. He gazed at her in wondering admiration and earned a friendly smile.

The smile faded when Lori turned to face the inspector. "What's the trouble?" she repeated.

Rodericks looked at her reflectively, taking his time about answering. "Do you know, I find that a strange question in this house today," he said at last. His voice deepened as he went on. "I would say that there is a great deal of trouble and that it involves all of you intimately. But to be more specific, I propose to interrogate Miss Weston and Dr. Bannister is objecting."

"Not objecting," said Bannister, "refusing permission on medical grounds."

Rodericks smiled at this, but the effect was chilling, a ray of Arctic sunlight on an ice field. "Mrs. Weston, would you be good enough to bring your stepdaughter down to me at once, please?"

Lori moved closer to Rodericks and looked up at him appealingly. "But Inspector, the poor girl is sound asleep. And she does need it so badly! If only you could have heard her a few hours ago I'm sure you would understand. I went over to see her at Mrs. Middleborough's early this morning before she woke. Even under the drug she sobbed and shuddered as though she was having one long nightmare. Now she's sleeping naturally. Couldn't you leave her for a little longer?"

It was prettily done but it had no effect on Rodericks. He acknowledged Lori's skill with a tight little smile, but shook his head.

"I'm sorry, Mrs. Weston. Too much time has elapsed already. I'm afraid I have no choice but to insist."

Lori set her chin and looked very determined. "I won't wake her up, Inspector, and that's final."

Rodericks let a lot of patience creep into his voice. He spoke as though to an unreasonable child. "Now, Mrs. Weston. Either you go up and get her or I shall have to go myself and place her under arrest. You wouldn't want that, would you?"

"Let me see your warrant," Lori demanded. "And what will you charge her with?"

"I don't need a warrant, Mrs. Weston. And I don't propose to charge her with anything. Merely to hold her as a material witness. And I'll only do that if you absolutely force me to."

"This is completely inhuman!" Bannister burst out. "I'll see that it is reported to the proper authorities."

Lori laid a small white hand on the doctor's arm.

"Thank you, George," she said, "but perhaps the inspector is right. We don't want to be the cause of Ann's getting arrested, do we?" She lifted her head as though she was listening for something and Rodericks heard a car door slam in front of the house. "I think this is a matter for a lawyer to handle. And that should be Mr. Castle arriving now. I sent for him before I came downstairs." She looked at Rodericks defiantly.

"Was this your own idea, Mrs. Weston?" he asked.

"Yes. Of course it was. Have you any objection?"

"None at all. I'm merely curious as to why you considered it necessary."

Lori bit her lip, displaying small, even teeth, then gave a little shrug. "Why beat around the bush like this?" she asked. "Ann is in trouble, isn't she? You suspect her of having killed Aileen. I know you do."

"Now, Mrs. Weston —" Rodericks began, but Lori went on.

"You had men searching everywhere for the gun last night — even at Mrs. Middleborough's. That means you think Ann hid it, that she took it with her across the street and hid it. She was the only one who could have taken it to Mrs. Middleborough's, wasn't she?"

"No," said Rodericks placidly. "As a matter of fact, no. The doctor could have taken it over there, for one. He was the first person present at the scene of the crime after your stepdaughter." As Bannister began to speak, the inspector held up his hand. "No one is suggesting that you did do this, Doctor. No one at all. I'm merely making a point. Or Mrs.

Middleborough now. She could conceivably have removed the revolver from the bathroom when she was in there being sick. People often hide things in the water tanks of toilets, you know. So, Mrs. Weston, you mustn't leap to conclusions. The revolver wasn't found at Mrs. Middleborough's, as a matter of fact. I didn't think it would be. But, of course, we had to look."

"I don't care what you say," Lori retorted. "Ann is still under suspicion and she has a right to a lawyer."

"Undoubtedly she has. But at this stage she is no more under suspicion than anyone else."

This was not quite true, Rodericks reminded himself. A part of his mind began to wonder, quite impersonally, how the assurance could have been rephrased so that the words would have been strictly true without being revealing.

Like a stage butler appearing on cue, Corporal Moore loomed up in the doorway of the drawing room. "There's a Mr. Castle here, sir. Says he's a lawyer representing the Weston family."

Castle was a big, florid man who looked as though he drank. He beamed genially at the four persons in the back parlor, but there was a sort of desperate intelligence in his little, blood-shot eyes. An odor of stale spirits lingered on his breath. Rodericks shook hands with him and introduced Sergeant Peele, then said,

"I understand Mrs. Weston asked you to come over."

"That is correct, sir, that is correct. A wicked business this, wicked. I'm here more as a friend of the family than as their legal representative. Known them all for years, haven't I, Lori? Well —" He looked around him, selected an armchair and sat down, breathing heavily. The others remained standing. "Well," he said again, "the question, I suppose, is how best we can all help the police, without — hmm — endangering anyone's health, eh?" He smiled his utterly false smile and darted quick little glances at each person in turn.

Rodericks missed the last part of what Castle was saying. From his position by the piano the inspector had a view of the hall and the back stairs, and coming slowly down those stairs, with one hand on the bannister as though for guidance and support, was Ann Weston.

9

THE LAWYER'S HEARTY VOICE died out uncertainly as he followed the inspector's gaze. Dr. Bannister and Mrs. Weston swung around and Sergeant Peele wrenched his eyes away from Lori. The back parlor become very still. For a moment no one moved except the slim dark girl coming hesitantly down the stairs.

Then Lori and Bannister went quickly forward and took up positions on either side of her. Mr. Castle struggled to his feet, wheezing a little as he did so. As Ann Weston entered the room, Rodericks saw that she was still pale and shaken, and he guessed from the droop of her eyelids that she had not yet entirely emerged from the influence of the sedative. She was fully dressed in a three-piece suit of light brown.

Lori was the first to speak, her voice sharp with protest, "She's not well enough to be questioned. Can't you see? She should be in bed."

Dr. Bannister, who was unobtrusively taking Ann's pulse, caught Rodericks' eye and frowned.

Castle bustled forward, seized Ann's right hand in both of his and made a funny little half-bow over it. "We must cooperate with the police, mustn't we?" he intoned in his fruity voice. "We have nothing to hide. Nothing whatsoever. But really, my dear, I must agree with your stepmother. You should be in bed. I'm sure the inspector understands."

"Nonsense," said Ann. "What are all of you trying to do? Of course I can talk to them now." She looked doubtfully at Peele, then at the inspector. "To you?"

Rodericks nodded. Ann moved over and sat in the chair that Castle had vacated. She glanced around her sleepily and stifled a yawn.

"We want whoever did it caught, don't we?" she said.

Rodericks' eyes flicked over Lori, Bannister and Castle in one quick searchlight sweep. None of them looked enthusiastic about Ann's suggestion. Ann seemed to notice this herself for she sat up straighter in the chair.

"You don't really think I could have done it, do you?" There was an edge of hysteria in her voice and Dr. Bannister laid a soothing hand on her shoulder. "Murdered Aileen? My own sister? You can't believe that! Or that anyone — the police — might think I would — simply because of the money —"

"No one has suggested anything of that sort, Miss Weston," said Rodericks, "but would you explain what you mean about the money?"

Ann nodded towards Castle. "Why hasn't he told you?" she asked. "It's just that Aileen's inheritance will come to me now." She shut her eyes and her face began to twitch. Her mouth twisted in an expression of grief and two large tears squeezed out from the corners of her eyes and slowly coursed down her cheeks.

Rodericks spoke very softly to her. "We do want the

murderer caught, Ann. And so there are some questions I must ask you."

She opened her eyes at his use of her first name and stared numbly at him.

"Perhaps you would prefer to talk to me alone, Ann," Rodericks went on. "Or, if you insist, with Mr. Castle present."

"I don't insist at all," said Ann. "I'll talk to you alone. I'd rather. Ask me anything you like. I don't care. All I care about is that Aileen's dead." She began to rock back and forth in the chair, her face contorted and her hands clenched tight. "I'll never see her again!" She buried her face in the back of the chair and her shoulders shook.

Rodericks had regarded this impassively, but now he looked up and spoke to the others. "You heard Miss Weston. I would appreciate it if you would all leave now. I will be as brief and as gentle as I can."

Castle opened his mouth, but caught Rodericks' eye, and closed it again. Lori, who had been watching the lawyer hopefully, saw his capitulation and her lips tightened. She looked at him with a flash of scorn in her eyes. For a moment it seemed that she might stand and fight it out, but the doctor put his hand on her arm as though to warn her that further resistance was useless. She and Bannister moved reluctantly toward the door and the lawyer followed them. Bannister turned before he went out and said, "I'll be in the next room. If she faints or becomes hysterical, call me at once. And I want you to know that I am holding you responsible for this."

Rodericks drew up a chair opposite Ann and motioned for Sergeant Peele to do the same. Peele put his hand inside his coat and half drew out his shorthand notebook but Rodericks gave a little negative shake of his head. The two men sat and waited. It was a full minute before Ann stopped shaking and looked up at them.

"When you're ready, Ann," Rodericks said kindly. "Take your time."

"I'm ready now."

"Then I think the best thing would be for you to tell me what happened, starting with the ringing of the doorbell. Try to remember everything you can."

Ann nodded and brushed a tear out of her eye. "All right. I'll try." She sat for a moment, twining her hands together so that the knuckles showed white. Rodericks noticed that on the third finger of her left hand she wore a medium-sized solitaire diamond, presumably Fred Dunn's engagement ring. She drew a deep, shuddering breath and spoke with a quaver in her voice. "It would have been about five minutes to six. It was quite dark outside and Lori had been gone for a few minutes. Aileen and I were sitting in the front room. Aileen was all ready to leave. She even had her coat on, but I was still in my slip. I was mending a glove, you see. If it hadn't been for that I might have been the one who answered the door."

She sobbed again, and Rodericks said, "You mustn't think about that. Just concentrate on what happened."

"When I heard the doorbell I got up and ran up the stairs. I had finished the glove anyway and had been just about to go."

"You went up the front stairs?"

"Yes. They were closer. My room is the second one along the upstairs hall from the front of the house. I ran up the stairs, but as I went I could see through the hall to the front door. It's frosted glass, you know. I could see the shape of someone outside."

"Could you tell what this person was wearing?"

Ann shook her head. "No. He was just a shape through the glass."

"You say 'he,' " Rodericks said. "Could you tell from the shape that it was a man?"

Again Ann shook her head but less certainly. "No," she said slowly. "No, it was just a shape. But it was a man."

"How do you know it was a man?"

"Because I saw him later on, leaving the house."

"That was the only thing that makes you think it was a man? I mean, you didn't know at the time?"

"No," said Ann slowly. "No. But I thought it was. I was upstairs and in my room by the time Aileen got to the door, but I could hear their voices. They were speaking very low. I thought perhaps it was Paul."

"Because of the sound of the voice or merely because they were talking low?" Rodericks asked.

"Because they were talking low. Aileen was in love, you know. I thought —"

Rodericks nodded. "Yes. I see. Then you couldn't tell from the voice whether it was a man or a woman?"

"No. No, I suppose not, but I assumed it was a man."

"Could you make out anything that was said?"

"No. Nothing. Not a word. Just the mutter of their voices — then they went into the front room and I didn't hear them any more."

"You weren't listening particularly?"

"No. Not particularly. I was hurrying to get dressed.

Aileen had been a little annoyed with me because I had kept her waiting. I put on my dress, and then —" She broke off and shivered violently.

"Before we come to that," Rodericks said, "can you tell me whether the front door was locked when your sister answered the bell?"

Ann thought for a second before replying. "I really can't say. It probably was. It's a spring lock and it's usually on. We all carry keys with us when we go out."

"So if the door had been locked and if Mrs. Weston had forgotten something — had to come back for it — she wouldn't have rung the bell but would have used her key?"

"Yes. Unless she had forgotten her key, of course. But she wouldn't do that. Lori never forgets anything." Ann broke off suddenly and looked up at Rodericks. "You're not suggesting — when you asked if it could have been a woman at the door — that's utterly ridiculous!"

"I'm not suggesting anything. Certainly not what you seem to think. But little points are often important — whether a door was locked or unlocked — things like that. I must try to form as accurate a picture as possible in my mind."

"Well," said Ann, "it sounded to me as though you might be suggesting that it was Lori who came back — who rang the bell. And it certainly wasn't! Lori —"

Rodericks interrupted firmly. "Please don't read more into my questions than is meant, Miss Weston. You were saying that you had put on your dress —"

"There were some shots. I don't know how many. More than one. And Aileen screamed." Ann's hands went up to her face and she began to rock back and forth again. "Oh God! How she screamed! It was awful. As though her mouth was full of blood!"

"Were there any shots after the scream?"

Ann took her hands away from her face and looked at the inspector. The horror in her eyes faded a little as she thought about the question. "Yes," she said. "Yes, there were. There was one shot first. Then the scream. Then more shots. Then I heard a thud. I knew it was her body falling to the floor. That's how it was."

"And what did you do then?"

"I just stood there. No. Wait. I opened my door and went out into the hall. I was too terrified to do anything. I just stood and shook."

"And then?"

Ann seemed to be looking inward when she spoke. Her voice was almost a whisper. "Everything was absolutely quiet. I cried out. Something, I don't know what. I don't know what I said. Then I heard sounds downstairs. As though someone had banged into a piece of furniture. Then I heard footsteps. They came out of the front room into the hall. Not hurrying but slow and heavy. They began to come up the stairs."

Her face went blank and she sat there with her mouth a little open, not speaking.

"Go on," Rodericks prompted her. "What did you do next?"

"I ran. That's it. I ran. Down the hall and down the back stairs. I didn't have my shoes on, you see, so I suppose I didn't make any noise. I went out through the dining room to the kitchen and out the back door. I closed the back door behind me. I remember doing that — very quietly so he wouldn't hear. Then I crept out along the wall through the snow to the back of the garden. I wanted to get out the back gate, you see, and escape that way. But I couldn't get it open." She looked down at her hands. Rodericks saw that the nail on her left forefinger was torn. "I couldn't get it open," she said again.

"Yes," said Rodericks. "I see. The snow was piled up against it, was it?"

"That's right. It moved a little but not enough. And I couldn't get over the wall. So I simply stayed there. I thought I was going to be killed. I thought he would come out and kill me." She paused and something of last night's fear seemed reflected on her face. "But he didn't. I waited for a long time — at least it seemed a long time — perhaps it wasn't really — and I began to get terribly cold. My feet were numb. Then I saw him cross the road in front of the house and go off down the other side of the street."

"What did he look like?" asked Rodericks.

She shook her head. "Just a shape. A shadow. I could tell it was a man but I couldn't really see him. He didn't go near the streetlight. He just disappeared."

"You are sure, though, that it was a man?"

"Why yes. He wore an overcoat and a hat. I'm sure he wore a hat."

Rodericks' experience told him that when a witness said "I'm sure" in that tone of voice, it meant that the first doubts had crept in.

"It couldn't have been a woman?" he asked. "Wearing an overcoat perhaps? Perhaps wearing a man's hat?"

Ann's doubts now were plain to read on her face. She said slowly, "I suppose it could have been a woman. I don't know."

The inspector was not unused to having evidence fade and dissolve in this manner, but it always saddened him. He said, "The man who followed you home on two occasions — you are sure that *he* was a man?"

Ann flushed. "Yes," she said in a stifled voice.

"Believe me, I am not being sarcastic. But if the person who frightened you last week was definitely a man, this might have preconditioned your mind. You might have unconsciously associated the incidents last week with what happened last night."

Ann's hands twisted together in her lap. "I don't know," she said.

"Your stepmother seemed to think you might have recognized the man who followed you, Miss Weston. Did you?"

"Lori said *that?"*

"She suggested it as a possibility."

Ann shook her head. "No," she said. "I did not recognize him. I did think though —"

"Yes?"

"Only that there was something familiar about him. As though I should have recognized him. I don't know — it was like a word that's on the tip of your tongue but you can't think of it."

"All right, Miss Weston," Rodericks said. "Don't worry about it for now. If anything occurs to you later, let me know immediately. Something may. Memory is like that. So if you should remember anything — anything at all, however trivial or unimportant it may seem to you — let me know at once. Now, you were in the back garden and you had just seen this person cross the road and disappear. What did you do next?"

"After a little while I began to think about Aileen — that she might still be alive. Though I knew she wasn't. Not after that scream. Anyway I went back in."

"That was very brave of you, when you might have gone off to get help first."

"I was thinking of Aileen," Ann said. "I had to see for myself. So I went back in."

"Yes?"

"And I found her. At the foot of the stairs." Ann began to tremble again.

"You hadn't seen your sister's body the first time? On your way out?"

Ann stared at him, her eyes wide. She shook her head mutely.

"Your sister's body was partly visible from the back stairs," Rodericks explained. "And it could be seen from the hall. But you didn't notice anything?"

"No," said Ann. "I suppose I wasn't looking. I was terrified, you know. I just ran down the stairs and out the back door."

Rodericks nodded. "So you came in and found your sister. Was she dead when you found her?"

"Oh yes. I think so. Yes, she was dead. She was all covered in blood and her poor mouth —" Ann began to sob, and the inspector reached out and took her hand.

"There now. I'm sorry. Please hold on just a little longer, Ann. There are a few more things I have to know."

The sobbing gradually died away and Ann raised her eyes.

"Don't misunderstand me, please," Rodericks said, "but how did you get on with your sister?"

"I loved her." The small hands clenched and unclenched in her lap.

Rodericks, remembering Lori Weston's slight hesitation when he had questioned her on this subject, decided to gamble. "There had been no quarrel, then?" he asked. "No disagreement?"

A fleeting reflection of some new emotion crossed Ann's face. Rodericks was not certain, but he thought it might be fear.

"Who told you?" she asked. "Who told you that?"

Rodericks evaded the question. "Tell me about it," he suggested.

"It wasn't really a quarrel. A disagreement, that's all it was. But I was rude to her. Oh God! I was rude to her that last day!"

"What was it about?"

"It's very involved," said Ann. She took a Kleenex out of the pocket of her jacket and blew her nose. "There's this boy, you see — Carl Fleury. I used to go out with Carl in high school. He had come to Farnham to live with his aunt after his parents died. We went — well, steady — for about four years. Aileen never liked Carl."

For the first time the look of sorrow on Ann's face faded. It was replaced with the faint shadow of something else. Rodericks was reminded of an expression he had sometimes seen on a child's face when it felt it had been treated unjustly by a parent — stubborn, resentful, and yet at the same time secretive.

"Carl was a bit wild, I suppose," Ann said. "Irresponsible. Anyway Aileen never liked him. It sort of spoiled things. She was older than I was, you see, and after mother died she — looked after me."

Ann stopped while the tears gathered in her eyes and ran silently down her cheeks. Rodericks sensed that these tears were not for her sister's death, or not for that alone. When she began to speak again the tears continued to flow but her voice was calm.

"Carl got into trouble and went away. He joined the army and went away."

"What kind of trouble?" asked Rodericks. He did not want to ask but he had to know.

"He hurt another boy in a fight. It was an accident really. Not Carl's fault. There were no charges laid or anything. But the boy died. Carl had knocked him down, you see, and he hit his head on a stone."

"All this happened — when?"

"Three years ago," said Ann. "I was only eighteen. Carl was nineteen. We were just kids." She looked back unbelievingly at eighteen from the vantage point of twenty-one. "Aileen wouldn't let me go out with him anymore, and people were pretty horrid, so he went away. We wrote to each other once in a while — he's been in Germany with the NATO brigade for the past two years."

She sniffed and dabbed at her eyes with her wet Kleenex. Rodericks took out a clean linen handkerchief and handed it to her. She took it absently and wiped her cheeks.

"This next bit is hard to explain," she said. "I don't think I understand it myself. But when Aileen said she was going to marry Paul, I felt I had to do something — get away. I couldn't stay on here with Dad and Lori all by myself. So I got engaged to Fred. It seemed like a good idea. He was fun to be with — made me laugh a lot. And Fred's clever. I'm not clever at all myself, but I like a boy who is. That was one of the things I always liked about Carl."

Sergeant Peele stirred restively in his chair but the inspector stilled him with a glance.

"I wrote to Carl at Christmas and told him about my engagement. When he didn't answer my letter I thought that that was the end of it. But a week ago he turned up here."

Sergeant Peele straightened, his interest reviving. Rodericks never took his eyes off Ann's face.

"He'd got leave, you see, and flew back from Germany with the air force. I've been seeing him, of course. And last Sunday Aileen found out about it. She didn't like it." Ann paused and then said a little lamely, "And that was what the disagreement was about."

"When did you last see Carl? Carl — Fleury?"

"Yesterday morning. We went roller-skating together. Because we used to, you see." It was something she found comforting to remember. Rodericks felt old and tired.

"How serious was this — disagreement?" he asked.

Ann began to cry quietly again. "Not really serious. Aileen didn't know — she thought I was being fickle — two-timing on Fred. She thought Carl was no good — just a sergeant in the army —" Then with a note of real despair "But she hardly spoke to me the last two days of her life!"

It was some time before Ann regained sufficient control of herself to go on. Rodericks and Peele sat awkwardly in their chairs with no help to offer. Doctors carried with them the gift of oblivion in ampules of Nembutal, but policemen, who sought justice and not healing, had only a further question. At last the inspector said:

"Does Mr. Dunn know anything about this?"

Ann shook her head. "I haven't told him yet. Nobody knew except Aileen. And Carl's aunt. I guess she knew."

"Oh, his aunt's still alive, is she?"

Ann looked surprised. "Why, yes. Of course. His aunt is Mrs. Middleborough. Carl used to live just across the street from me."

The inspector did not comment on this. His next question struck in smoothly at a tangent, "A little while ago you said something about inheriting money from your sister. Would you mind explaining that?"

"Mr. Castle could do it better, I think," Ann said wearily. "But it's simple really. Mother had money of her own — quite a lot of money. When she died most of it was left to Aileen and me in trust. We were to get it when we were twenty-five or when we married. Whichever came first. If one of us died, the whole fund went to the other."

"I see," said Rodericks. After a moment he added, "An unusual will."

"Father had a good job of his own," Ann explained. "He is the head of the Thameside Laboratories. And he got the house and furniture."

And to my husband, thought Rodericks, my second-best bed. But who can tell me about this? Not Ann Weston, I think. And Castle won't, even if he knows. Mrs. Weston perhaps — it may be a sore point with her.

"And now there is just one thing more," he said. "I've

kept you too long as it is. Dr. Bannister will be annoyed with me, I'm afraid. But I understand that yesterday afternoon, just before the doorbell rang, there was a telephone call to this house. Is that right?"

"Two calls," said Ann. "There were two telephone calls just before six o'clock. One right after the other."

Rodericks showed no surprise. "Tell me about them," he suggested.

"Aileen answered the phone both times. She was sitting with her coat on, you see, waiting for me to get my glove mended and get dressed."

"The calls were for your sister?"

"No, they were both for Lori, but she had left. I don't know who called the first time. The second time it was Molly Fitzpatrick."

"The first caller didn't identify himself?" Rodericks asked.

"I don't know. Aileen might have told me but the phone rang again as soon as she hung up. Molly wanted to borrow our ice bucket, but Lori had already taken it."

"So you have no idea who the first caller was?"

"No. How could I have?"

"Well, sometimes you can guess from hearing only one side of a conversation, can't you? Even when no names are mentioned."

"I wasn't paying much attention, I'm afraid. Aileen answered and said that no, Lori had gone."

"Didn't she say anything else? I would like you to try to remember, if you can. It might be important."

"Why should it be important?" Ann asked.

Rodericks had already decided not to answer this question if it were asked. At least not yet. In any case, it was only a guess — a guess that the first telephone call might have been from someone who had wanted to make sure that Aileen Weston was home that afternoon. Or that Lori Weston was not. He said, "Can't you recall anything else your sister said?"

Ann frowned in concentration. "Now, wait. Yes. I remember that Aileen said something like, 'Well, if Ann ever gets dressed in time, we are.' I think she meant that we were going to the party. Then she laughed, but she sounded sort of exasperated too. She had been ready quite a while and was tired of waiting for me."

When she had said this, Ann's face suddenly crumpled. "Oh, God!" she cried bitterly. "I never thought of it before, but if I hadn't been so slow —" She began to tremble again.

Rodericks put his hand on her shoulder.

"I don't think it would have made any difference," he said. "No difference at all. You mustn't distress yourself."

Dr. Bannister spoke from the doorway.

"She's not distressing herself. You are doing that and very competently. And I insist that you stop it, for the time being at least."

He came into the room and Lori Weston followed him. Both of them looked indignant. Rodericks and Peele stood up and watched in silence while Ann was led out.

"It's a rotten job," said Peele.

Rodericks did not answer him. He was thinking about the first telephone call.

10

THERE WERE FOUR PEOPLE in the dining room when Rodericks and Peele entered. Mr. Castle was sitting at the head of the mahogany table, looking like the seedy patriarch of some rather disreputable clan. On opposite sides of the table but at some distance down from the lawyer were Anstruthers and Dunn. Dunn was scowling behind his glasses and there was a malicious smile on Anstruthers' face.

Leaning negligently against the sideboard was a tall black-haired man in khaki battledress with a sergeant's stripes on his sleeves. The soldier was immaculate, his uniform smartly pressed, his puttees a miracle of smoothness, his brass belt buckle and shoulder flashes gleaming, his black boots brilliant. His swarthy face under straight black eyebrows contained a hint of recklessness and the way he carried himself revealed more than a hint of self-confidence. Even in repose he had a swashbuckling air. Rodericks thought that he looked like a gypsy or a pirate.

Rodericks nodded to the soldier, "Sergeant Fleury? I'm glad you're here. It saves me the trouble of sending for you. I'm Inspector Rodericks of the Ontario Provincial Police. This is Sergeant Peele. Just take a chair there, if you would. I'll get around to you in a minute."

Fleury moved lightly and gracefully to sit down next to Anstruthers. He did not seem in the least put out by the inspector's tone.

Rodericks addressed himself to Castle. "And now, sir, there are a few small matters I'd like you to clear up for me, if you would."

Castle stirred ponderously. "Would it not be better, Inspector, if this interview were conducted in private?"

"I'll talk to you privately later," Rodericks replied. "At the moment I want to clear the air a little."

Castle's small, shrewd eyes darted quickly from Dunn to Anstruthers and back to the inspector. "Very well. Although, naturally I reserve the right to protect my clients' interests by not answering whenever I see fit."

"You have known the Westons for some time, Mr. Castle?"

"For many years. Dr. Weston has lived in Farnham for at least two decades and I have been the family lawyer throughout that period. Also, I think I may say, a personal friend."

"You have known the present Mrs. Weston for a somewhat shorter time?"

"Five years," Castle replied, a trifle curtly.

"That would be since her marriage?"

Castle nodded. "Lori worked in London before she married Bob Weston. They met there, got married and moved into this house."

"In your opinion were the members of the Weston family on good terms with one another?"

"Excellent, I would say. I know what you're getting at, of course, but in this case there was, so far as I know, never the slightest ill-feeling between the two girls and their stepmother. Often there is, I grant you. But Lori Weston is a most remarkable woman. Everyone likes her. And as far as my own observation goes I should say that she was like an older sister to Aileen and Ann."

Dr. Bannister came down the back stairs. He still looked angry but he went along the hall without a glance into the dining room. Rodericks found himself waiting for the front door to slam. After a moment it did.

The inspector let his glance rest on Paul Anstruthers, but when he spoke again he still addressed the lawyer. "Now, Mr. Castle, would you tell us please, what are the financial implications of Miss Aileen Weston's death? As regards inheritance."

"I don't know that I ought to answer that question," Castle said slowly. "However, since it is certain to become public knowledge very soon, I will do so. In general terms, Inspector."

He's as anxious as I am to see what reaction there will be, Rodericks thought. Anstruthers and Dunn were both leaning slightly forward to catch the lawyer's words. Carl Fleury took out a cigarette and lit it.

"To the best of my knowledge and belief," said Castle, rounding his words as though he enjoyed them, "Miss Aileen Weston died intestate." He glanced patronizingly down the table to Fleury. "That means without having made a will."

Fleury bowed gravely. "Thank you," he said, and Castle flushed.

Anstruthers spoke sharply. "Are you sure of that?" he demanded. "She told me she was going to." His voice was shrill and indignant.

"She consulted me on the subject," Castle admitted. "I advised her to wait until after her marriage which, I understand, was to have been in April. Under the circumstances, I saw no point in her making a will 'in contemplation of marriage,' and since any other form of will would have been invalidated by her marriage, it seemed only sensible to postpone it until April. Naturally, I had no idea —"

"You damned interfering old bastard!" said Anstruthers in a vicious whisper.

Rodericks struck the table top with the flat of his hand.

"That will be enough of that, Mr. Anstruthers!" he said in a voice that cracked like a whip.

The red blotches on the lawyer's face turned slowly purple as he glared at Anstruthers, but Rodericks kept control of the situation. "Please go on, Mr. Castle."

With an effort Castle turned back to the inspector and saw the cold twinkle in his eye. He spluttered a little but continued with his statement. "Under the terms of the late Mrs. Weston's will, the monies that Aileen Weston would have inherited revert to the trust fund in sole benefit of her sister, Ann Weston."

Fred Dunn ran a pink tongue along the outside of his lower lip. "How much money is involved, sir?" he asked.

Castle regarded him coldly. "I see no reason for divulging that information." He looked at Rodericks and added, "I'll tell you privately if you like. It will be only a rough estimate, mind you. There are considerable stock holdings that would have to be evaluated."

Carl Fleury spoke for the first time. "I would like to point out right now that Ann had no need of this extra money. Her own portion was more than enough for her."

Anstruthers twisted in his chair to look at Fleury. His eyes narrowed and the malice on his face was unmistakable. "Some people hold that you can never have enough money," he said. "I'm not suggesting, of course, that Ann is one of them. But I'm sure the extra windfall from Aileen's death will be very welcome to Ann's future husband." He smiled brightly, showing his teeth. "Whoever that may be," he added.

Rodericks looked around the table, gathering eyes. "Thank you very much, gentlemen. That will be all for now. Mr. Castle, I'll call in at your office later today if I may."

They scraped back their chairs and stood up. Rodericks said, "Oh, I'd like you to wait, if you would, Sergeant Fleury."

Fleury sat down again. His expression was ironical as he watched Castle, Dunn and Anstruthers walk out of the room.

"You flew back from Germany, Sergeant? About a week ago?"

"Exactly a week ago," said Fleury. "I landed in Canada on the eighth."

"And came directly to Farnham?"

"Where else? I've got thirty days' leave. I arrived here on the morning of the ninth."

"Miss Weston seems to think you returned because of a letter she wrote you at Christmas."

"On the fourth of January actually," said Fleury. "I didn't get it until the ninth. Then it took some time to arrange a booking on an air force flight. And yes, that's why I came back."

He stopped as though waiting for another question, but

Rodericks sat quiet. Fleury continued, "I expect you've heard about it from Ann. I'm the poor orphan boy from next door. Ann and I grew up together and I have intended to marry her for as long as I can remember. Perhaps I should have made that clearer to her before. Then there wouldn't have been any of this nonsense with that little runt Dunn. But she understands now all right."

"You have a dominating personality, Sergeant," said Rodericks.

"Meaning, I suppose, that I'll bully her into marrying me. Probably because I want her money. Also meaning — perhaps — that I'm the type who might not take kindly to an older sister's interference. Possibly that I might have killed the older sister to put a stop to that interference."

Rodericks made no comment, but continued to look at Fleury steadily.

"All right," said Fleury. "I'll bully her into marrying me — if I have to. But I won't have to. She's loved me as long as I've loved her. And that was long before I knew her mother was rich. As to Aileen, it's true we never got along. The truth was she was jealous. Not of me particularly. It would have been the same with anyone who was fond of Ann. Aileen was an old maid before her time. That's how she came to be taken in by that queer, Anstruthers."

"An interesting theory," said Rodericks dryly. "Have you by any chance got an alibi for last night?"

"No, I have not." Fleury was completely unperturbed. "I went up to London yesterday afternoon and got caught by the storm. I was in no hurry to get back anyway. Mrs. Fitzpatrick is a fine, upstanding woman but she doesn't invite army sergeants to her cocktail parties."

"You've got a chip on your shoulder," the inspector told him. "I expect she'd have asked you like a shot if she had known you were in town. So you stayed in London overnight?"

"I did. I slept in the sergeants' quarters at Wolseley Barracks as a matter of fact."

"And signed the book?"

"And signed the book. But it won't help me. I didn't sign in until a quarter to twelve — plenty of time to have run back to Farnham, committed a murder or two and returned to London."

Rodericks sighed. "All right. Where did you go? From about five-thirty on."

"I had dinner at a restaurant. I don't know what it's called and it was so crowded they wouldn't remember me anyway —"

"Were you in uniform?" Rodericks asked.

"No. In civvies. I told you they wouldn't remember me."

"People have been hanged because of that attitude," Rodericks told him. "They don't do that any more in these tender-hearted days, but they can still lock you up for a long, long time."

"Not for so long, Inspector. It would unduly delay the murderer's rehabilitation. And I'm on your side about that. The restaurant was a German one on Dundas Street."

"Feldmann's?"

"That's it. I got in there about a quarter to six, had dinner, left by half past six and went to a show. I don't know the name of the theater but the movie was *Camelot*. Personally, I liked the book better."

"A lot of people said that," Rodericks assured him.

"We'll check on the restaurant, of course. What did you do after the show?"

"The sergeants' mess. Two slow beers and then to bed. I didn't hear about the murder until I got back to my aunt's this morning. Ann had already left, so I haven't seen her yet — not since Aileen was killed."

"Right," said Rodericks. "That's all for now."

They both stood up. Fleury nodded and started for the door. Before he got there he turned back.

"One more thing," he said. "For what it's worth. I'm captain of the Third Brigade's pistol shooting team. We came first in the NATO competitions last year."

He went out, as straight as a ramrod.

"A fine body of men, Colonel," said Sergeant Peele. "A fine body of men."

"Dunn wouldn't seem to have much chance against that sort of competition," Rodericks agreed. "But the motive's there, you know. And there is a history of violence. I must look that up, by the way. Or better still, *you* look it up. There would have been an inquest. And Ted, while you're about it, you can drop in and see Castle at his office. I want to know how much money is involved. And try to find out if there is anything else he can tell us. I'm going to the hospital to fight with Dr. Bannister."

"Is that where he went? To the hospital?"

"I imagine so. He won't want to see me again. Have you noticed, Ted, that no one in this case seems to like the police very much?"

"You mean you're going to talk to Dr. Weston?"

"I'm going to try. I don't put my chances very high."

While they had been talking, Rodericks and Peele had

walked out through the back parlor and the drawing room to the front hall. As they were putting on their coats, Constable Holmsted appeared behind them. He cleared his throat and stood there awkwardly.

Rodericks fixed him with a cold eye. "Ah, Constable. I see you shaved this morning. My congratulations. Did you want to speak to me?"

Holmsted looked sullen but said, "Yes, sir. It's Corporal Moore, sir. He phoned from the office. There's a Mrs. Falls down there who wants to make a statement."

"She should be encouraged to do so," said Rodericks. "Have you any idea of the substance of this statement? I take it it's concerned with our murder."

"Yes, sir. It seems that Mrs. Falls was walking down Maple Street last night, past this house. She heard three pistol shots come from inside. She thought it strange but didn't do anything about it until she heard the eight o'clock news this morning. Then she drove into Farnham to report it. She lives out in the country, sir, at Hartmann's Corners."

"And did she have anything to say about the time at which this happened?"

"She said it was five past six, sir, by her watch."

"Another job for you, Ted," said Rodericks. "You're earning your pay this morning. Go down and take Mrs. Falls' statement. It's only confirmatory evidence but every little bit helps."

"If it was five past six, that would likely be the first series of shots, wouldn't it?" said Peele. "Do you know, it's a funny thing."

"What's a funny thing?"

"Well, only that no one seems to have heard the second

group of shots fired. The ones that actually killed her. I know there wouldn't be many people out on the streets on a night like that, but Miss Weston was supposed to be in the garden. You'd think *she'd* have heard something."

Rodericks only grunted in reply. They went out the front door and paused for a moment on the verandah. On the snow-covered street before the house stood Anstruthers and Dunn, apparently in heated dispute with Sergeant Fleury. The inspector pushed open the verandah door in the hope of hearing what was being said.

"— nothing but a bloody fortune-hunter." Dunn was almost chattering with rage.

The sergeant seemed to be listening politely, his head inclined a little forward toward the smaller man. Rodericks reflected that Fleury was the only soldier he had ever seen who managed to look positively glamorous in an issue greatcoat. He must have had it specially tailored, for it narrowed in at the waist and flared out dashingly in the skirts like the coat of a Tsarist cavalry officer. As the policemen watched, Fleury put out both his arms. He did it smoothly, in one rippling motion that had no sign of hurry about it. One gloved hand grasped Anstruthers by the collar; another seized Dunn. Their heads came together with a whack that could be plainly heard on the verandah. Sergeant Fleury strolled across the road, carrying himself as though he was on parade.

"So much for Rosencrantz and Guildenstern," breathed Rodericks. He softly closed the verandah door and stepped back a pace.

"I didn't see anything," said Sergeant Peele.

"No more did I," said Rodericks. "No more did I."

11

Simply by looking at the building and grounds an observant stranger would have said that Farnham was proud of its hospital. Rodericks' car swept up a curving, tree-lined drive which a snowplow had already cleared that morning. The white clapboard front of the hospital glistened with fresh paint, the windowpanes were sparkling clean and at the main entrance the brass plaque which immortalized the names of benefactors had been recently polished. In spite of appearances, Rodericks doubted the justification of Farnham's civic pride for he knew that, although the hospital served a wide area of countryside and several smaller villages, it had a capacity of only twenty beds. Long waiting lists and overcrowding would be chronic problems.

A commissionaire at the desk in the lobby directed Rodericks to the second floor. He went up by the stairs, smelling the clean, ominous hospital smell and experiencing the perceptible lowering of the spirits that these places always induced in him.

Surely it was a sign of age that he thought the floor nurse absurdly young for her job. She was a pretty, dark girl in a starched white uniform and the smile with which she greeted him was uncompromisingly professional. She was doubt-proof and sure of herself, with a conviction based on unchallengeable absolutes.

"Dr. Weston is still on our critical list. He is not allowed any visitors. I'm sorry."

Knowing that he would have to appeal her ruling, Rodericks still felt compelled to justify himself to her.

"It's very important. I'm investigating a murder. Possibly vital evidence."

The phrases meant nothing to her. The suppression of crime, the protection of society, all the urgent affairs of men had been weighed in her balance and found to count for nothing in comparison with the relief of pain, the healing of the sick, the preservation of life. Rodericks had to remind himself that he too had considered these things and had formed another opinion.

"May I see Dr. Bannister, please?"

Her bright smile faded. "He's in with the patient now. I don't know how long he will be."

Against the wall, away from the nurse's desk, there were two plain wooden chairs and an ashtray on a stand. Rodericks walked over and sat on one of the chairs. The nurse came out from behind her desk and looked down at him.

"Dr. Bannister has been here most of the night, working like a slave," she said. "If it hadn't been for him, Dr. Weston would have died shortly after he was admitted. It's still doubtful whether or not he will pull through. You would upset him. You can't want to do that."

Rodericks looked past her. Down the hall a door opened and Bannister, clad in a white coat, came out of a room, carefully shutting the door behind him. He began to walk along the hall toward the floor nurse's desk.

Rodericks stood up and waited for him to approach. Bannister nodded to him.

"I thought I might find you here." He put his hands in the pockets of his white smock and stared at his feet. "Weston's a very sick man," he said, "but I think he is going to be all right for the time being. He has been asking for you, as a matter of fact."

Bannister took his hands out of his pockets. There were new lines on his youthful face and his big frame seemed to droop with weariness but he displayed none of the hostility he had shown earlier that morning over Ann Weston.

"I'm going to let you in to see him. It's probably the lesser of two evils, for he is fretting about the killer not being caught. I think he is afraid for Lori and Ann. Try to reassure him. And don't dwell on any of the details of Aileen's death — not that they aren't on his mind in any case. I'll give you five minutes." He smiled suddenly, a little rueful smile that had a good deal of charm in it. "Not that I give a damn about your investigation. My patient is what counts, and I think you may do him more good than harm."

"I want to see him alone," Rodericks said.

Bannister nodded. "All right. But you'll have to watch him closely and use your common sense. If he seems to be in any pain, call me at once. I'll be here." He sat down heavily in one of the visitors' chairs and stretched his legs out in front of him. "Ask the nurse to wait outside."

Dr. Weston lay on his back on the narrow hospital bed that came up level with Rodericks' waist. Delicate frost patterns misted the inside of the storm window, but a patch of winter sunlight lay across the foot of the bed and weakly brightened half the floor of the little room. A dozen hot-house daffodils in a vase by the bedside drooped their pale yellow heads and seemed to repeat the motif of feeble suns and killing frosts.

Weston did not move or turn his head but his eyes followed the inspector as he crossed the room. Rodericks stood and looked down at the sick man. He was struck again, as he had been when he had seen them both in the photograph, by the strong resemblance between Ann Weston and her father. It was apparent now despite the waxen pallor of the man's face, his bloodless lips and sunken eyes. There were two small wet patches on the pillow slip which indicated that Dr. Weston had been crying.

"You are the man who is going to catch my daughter's murderer." Weston's voice was little more than a whisper, but what he said was a statement, not a question. Irrationally, Rodericks found himself believing it.

"Things fall into a pattern, Inspector. I can't see all of it yet, but it's there. You won't be able to see all of it either." Weston's eyes shifted away from Rodericks' face and regarded the sunlight on the coverlet. "Evil brings evil in unexpected ways."

He is not talking to me, Rodericks thought. I just happen to be here. He stood silent, eavesdropping.

"This pattern began eight years ago," Weston said. "On the seventh of June. That was the night I met Lori and fell in love with her. It was not her fault. She was too beautiful, that's all. I can't help thinking that some things are badly planned or happen by accident. She is really a very ordinary woman, although no one would believe it to look at her. It's as though the wrong spirit had been poured into her body. Beauty like hers should not be given by chance. It's too dangerous a gift." A hint of a smile touched the pale lips. "It never spoiled Lori though, as it does most women. She was still able to love, although not enough. Or long enough."

He shut his eyes and was silent for a time. Rodericks could hear the muted sounds outside the room, a car passing in the street, footsteps in the corridor. Below him on the bed Weston fingered the hours of his life like a rosary of sorrowful mysteries. At last he opened his eyes and began to speak again.

"Men make her love them," he said. "I did. Without thinking about the consequences. I wasn't a young man even then. I didn't have that excuse. She had had lovers before, of course, and she had one then. I ignored all that, asked no questions, wanted to hear no answers. It was two years before my wife died. It took that long to kill her. If it did kill her. Sometimes I think I blame myself too much — for things that might have happened anyway."

The silence came down again and Rodericks thought it best not to break it. So far he had heard nothing he had not guessed before, but there would be more to come.

"That was the reason for the will, of course. You must have wondered about the will, Inspector. Mary didn't believe in divorce. And she kept hoping that my affair with Lori would come to an end. I was fifteen years older, and I suppose it might have happened that way if Mary hadn't died."

Tears trickled out slowly from the corners of the tortured eyes, ran unheeded down the white cheeks. "She just got tired and died. But it did happen that way in fact. Too late.

Mary's dead, and without knowing that I loved her best. How could she know? I didn't know myself."

After a moment or two the tears ceased to fall and Weston looked at the inspector again.

"The will was part of the trouble. Especially with Aileen. She was never as pretty as Ann and I think she knew — somehow — about Lori and me. It changed her."

Rodericks ventured a question. "How did the will come into it?"

"It kept the best boys away," Weston said. "Not the money itself but how Aileen would have used the money. They didn't want to be tied to their wife's purse strings, and they thought they would be. None of that mattered to Anstruthers, of course. It was always the money with him. But you couldn't tell Aileen that."

"You think the money that your daughter would have inherited was the reason for her murder?"

"No, Inspector. I didn't say that. What I said was that it was all part of the same pattern. And that I am the one who is responsible. I set in motion the whole train of events."

"You are being hard on yourself," Rodericks told him, without conviction.

"Not that there was any trouble at home after my second marriage," Weston said as though he had not heard him. "Everyone gets along with Lori. They can't help it. There was a little tension at first, but no one can quarrel with Lori. And she was genuinely fond of the girls."

"Have you any suspicions?" asked Rodericks. "Any guesses?"

"No guesses," said Weston. "If I had I'd tell you. I don't know any names or I would say them. I'm in no position to stand on ceremony or to worry about being fair. I had my time for that and I failed."

For a moment or two he retreated again into his private world of remorse, forgetful of the policeman's presence. Then he said, "Anstruthers and Dunn are out for the money. Aileen missed that anyway. And Ann won't go through with it. She'll marry that boy from across the street. He's not much good but at least he doesn't care whether she's rich or poor. Anyway, Ann will be all right. She's like me. Too much like me. But she's tough. Aileen was the vulnerable one. Aileen and Lori. But Lori most of all. God knows what will happen to her now."

He turned his face to the wall and shut his eyes. Rodericks stayed by the bed for a time but Dr. Weston made no move and seemed to be asleep. There were in any case no questions Rodericks could think to ask. The antiseptic smell of the hospital was cloying in his nostrils. Outside the window an icicle dislodged itself from the eaves and fell, clattering against the wall. He had turned away from the bed and started toward the door when Dr. Bannister put his head inside the room and motioned for him to leave.

"You had more than five minutes," the doctor whispered. "How did he seem?"

"Sad," said Rodericks.

"Was he of any help to you?"

"Oh yes. Yes, he was of help to me. Anytime anyone talks it's of help to me. But I doubt if I was able to be of any help to him. It wasn't reassurance from me he needed."

Bannister went into the sick room, followed by the special duty nurse, and Rodericks went down the hall. The young floor nurse pretended to be busy with her charts and affected not to see him. He found the police car waiting in front of the hospital.

"Back to Maple Street," he told the driver, and relaxed in his seat to think over what Weston had said. One thing that occurred to him was that more people knew of Carl Fleury's return to Farnham than Ann had supposed. After a minute he leaned forward and rolled down the window. The smell of the hospital seemed to be clinging to him.

Sergeant Peele was in the dining room with his shorthand notebook on the table in front of him. Rodericks unbuttoned his overcoat but kept it on. He sat down opposite Peele.

"Well?"

"Nothing much," Peele said. "There's a lot of money involved. Castle thinks upwards of $350,000 in the trust. Each girl would have got $175,000. Now Ann Weston gets it all. In a year or two, Castle says, it will be worth a good bit more. Maybe half a million."

"Anything else?"

"Not from Castle. If he has any ideas, he's keeping them to himself. But I went on to the station. Mrs. Falls had gone back to Hartmann's Corners, and believe it or not, she hasn't got a telephone. However, Corporal Moore had taken a very full statement."

"Damn," said Rodericks. "All right, what did she say? We'll have to talk to her ourselves, of course, but that can wait until later today or tomorrow."

Sergeant Peele opened his notebook and thumbed through the pages. "Mrs. Falls heard three shots, at five past six. She checked the time, or so she says. She was right in front of this house when she heard them."

"She was on foot, was she?"

"Yes. She and her husband had come in from the farm to spend the day with their married daughter and do some shopping. The husband had the car somewhere — at the beer parlor, if you ask me, although she wouldn't say so — so while she was waiting for him to return she decided to drop over to Dr. Bannister's to see him about this pain she had been having in her back. It was on her way back from his surgery that she heard the shots."

"Did she recognize them for shots at the time?"

"Moore asked her that," Peele replied, "She said she did."

"Then why, in heaven's name —?"

"She's apparently not very bright," said Peele. "She thought it sufficiently peculiar to make a note of the time but then she didn't think anything more about it until she heard the news on the radio this morning."

Rodericks shrugged. "All right. What about Fleury?"

"There was a police report. He seems to be in the clear. A kid fight with fists. Behind the high school. And the other kid was older, bigger and heavier than Fleury. It was just bad luck that when he went down he hit his head on a rock."

"There were witnesses?"

"About twenty. You know what those fights are like. They all said the same thing."

"Anything on the cause of the fight?"

"That was a bit vague," Peele replied. "Something the other kid said, I gather. It never came out in the investigation."

"It probably doesn't matter. Now, look, Ted. You'll have to run things here for the rest of the day. I'm going in to London."

Peele raised his eyebrows. "Oh?"

"No. Nothing definite. But I want to talk to the crown

attorney. I think he should be briefed on the case right now. I'm not going to ask for a warrant and I don't want one yet."

"He may want you to arrest Ann Weston," said Peele.

Rodericks shook his head. "There's not nearly enough evidence for that. Even a lawyer like Castle could kill the case before it got to a jury. No, I just want to fill him in on the details. We've still a long way to go."

Corporal Moore stopped Rodericks in the drawing room.

"Two things, sir," he said. "First, no luck at all on the revolver. They've done the whole search again and not turned up a thing. Or rather they've turned up quite a collection of old iron of various sorts but no murder weapon."

Rodericks nodded. "Then it probably isn't there."

"No, sir. The second thing is, Miss Weston wants to see you. She's in the upstairs sitting room."

The inspector turned back and went up the big curving staircase. The sitting room was on the right at the head of the stairs. He knocked and went in.

Ann Weston was in an armchair by the window and Carl Fleury was standing beside her.

"How did you get in here?" Rodericks demanded.

"I walked in the back door and came up the back stairs," Fleury replied cheerfully. "Why not? Not counting this morning, it's the first time I've been in this house since I got back from Germany, but Ann was glad to see me."

He touched her shoulder and smiled down at her. She smiled back, a little uncertainly, but reached up with her left hand to cover his. The inspector noticed that Dunn's engagement ring was no longer on her finger.

"I'm sure she was glad to see you," Rodericks said, "but just the same I think I'll talk to Miss Weston alone."

Fleury straightened and met the inspector's eye. "Sure," he said. "Only don't bully her. I'll be outside in the hall. I know all about the rights of witnesses."

"Get out," said Rodericks, but he did not sound annoyed.

Fleury stooped, kissed Ann lightly on the forehead and walked out without another look at the inspector.

"You wanted to see me?"

"It's not important really," said Ann. "And Carl could have stayed to hear it. Why were you horrid to him?"

"I didn't think I was," said Rodericks. "But, tell me, was that right, what he said just now — that today was the first time he has been in this house since he got back to Farnham?"

"Why yes. We didn't want to cause any trouble. To annoy Aileen. I met him at his aunt's when we went out together."

"Natural enough, I'm sure. Now what have you got to tell me?"

"I wouldn't have bothered except you did say that if I remembered anything, however trivial —"

"I said it," Rodericks admitted, "and I meant it. You've remembered something?"

"I know it's silly," said Ann, "and it has nothing to do with the murder." She paused as though reluctant to continue.

"Tell me," Rodericks suggested.

"Well, I feel foolish bothering you with it. But do you know whether Corporal Moore got a comic Valentine?"

Rodericks stared at her.

"A pretty nasty one, I think it must have been. Aileen said it looked just like him in a horrid sort of way."

"Aileen told you this? How did she know?"

"She saw Constable Holmsted buying it last Saturday. In a store in London. He didn't see her because she ducked back out of sight, but after he had gone Aileen came out again and looked in the rack. There was one more left — the same as the one he had bought, I mean. Aileen said it couldn't possibly be for anybody except Corporal Moore."

"Your sister knew it was Constable Holmsted, did she? She identified him by name?"

"Oh yes, Inspector. Aileen and Bill Holmsted went to school together. He used to be a bit of a nuisance as a matter of fact — asking her to go out with him and not taking no for an answer. That was years ago, of course. Only that was why Aileen didn't want him to see her in the bookstore. He always kept her talking for so long, and, really, she couldn't stand him."

Somewhat dazedly Rodericks thanked her. At the head of the stairs Carl Fleury was waiting. They looked at each other without noticeable affection.

"You'll find her safe and well," said Rodericks. "I didn't have to use my thumb-screw even once."

Downstairs he sought out Corporal Moore.

"I hear you got a special Valentine this year, Corporal," he said when he found him. "May I see it?"

Moore stared at him for a moment in bewilderment. Then, reluctantly, he fished in his tunic pocket and produced the Valentine. Rodericks inspected it without comment and put it in his own pocket.

"I'll be back in about six hours," was all he said. "Keep an eye on things."

12

THE ELEVATOR that took the inspector up to the seventeenth floor where the crown attorney had his offices seemed to be both stationary and completely silent. Rodericks was willing to believe that mechanical ingenuity accounted for the illusion that he was not moving but he had a nagging suspicion that the elevator must make some sound. Perhaps at forty-eight his hearing was not as good as it should be. He forced himself to turn away from this morbidly fascinating train of thought and concentrate on his coming interview.

At thirty-four Harrison Gilbert was relatively young to be crown attorney of Middlesex County. His appointment had been evidence of ability, ambition and the possession of influential friends. Three good things to have, Rodericks reminded himself. He reminded himself too that he liked Gilbert and found him easy to work with. But the man had a sharp lawyer's mind, logical and precise, and he would take pleasure in catching the inspector out. Rodericks was amiably resolved to deny him this satisfaction.

The crown attorney's office was large and impersonal, like

Gilbert himself. It was bright with fluorescence, obtrusively air-conditioned and carpeted with wall-to-wall broadloom. The only decoration was an immense geometrical jumble in a frame on one wall. Harrison Gilbert sat behind a huge desk whose glass top was absolutely bare. Horn-rimmed glasses and a receding hairline helped him look serious and older than he was.

He waved Rodericks to a chair and from a drawer produced a manila folder that contained a typescript of Sergeant Peele's notes on the Weston case. He got down to business at once.

"John, I know that you will have omitted no relevant detail from this," indicating the folder, "so I don't propose to go over it step by step now. First of all, you had better bring me up to date. Peele's notes take me up to about last midnight. What's happened today?"

Rodericks told him, succinctly but thoroughly. Gilbert listened in silence, then said, "What I would like to do is to review the case with you — go over the evidence and the possibilities. That should let us see where we stand. We should make a good team on this one, you and I. We always have in the past. The logic of the law, and — what, thirty years — experience on the force. Logic and experience together should get us somewhere, don't you think?"

Rodericks wondered if Harrison Gilbert had heard the dictum of Chief Justice Oliver Wendell Holmes of Massachusetts that the life of the law was not logic but experience. He found the saying a comforting one, but thought it wiser not to quote it.

"So if it's all right with you," Gilbert went on, "I'd like to take the suspects in order and summarize the pros and cons of the evidence against them."

"Just as you like, sir. Will you start or shall I?"

"I think it might be better if I did. I've made some notes of my own and I'll follow them. Now — first — let's consider the possibility that Aileen Weston was murdered by someone who doesn't appear in this summary of evidence. And let's assume that this unknown murderer was the same man who followed the girls on two occasions and who attempted to break into the Weston house on Monday night."

Rodericks, who wanted to see how the crown attorney would proceed from there, said nothing. Gilbert peered over the top of his glasses, inviting comment, but when none came he went on, although less confidently.

"In favor of this hypothesis we have the evidence that a break-in was actually attempted and we have evidence that a man did follow the girls. The murder, coming as it did the day after the attempted break-in, is almost certain to be connected with it. To consider otherwise would be to place altogether too much faith in coincidence."

"If we look closely at this evidence, however, it doesn't seem very convincing," Rodericks pointed out. "There was a pane of glass broken in the kitchen window and there were some chisel marks on the window frame. Also some footprints in the snow under the window. I doubt if we are justified in speaking of an attempted break-in. It would be more accurate to speak of a simulated break-in."

"Very well. I agree entirely. But what about the man the girls saw?"

"There is one peculiar point about that story, sir. I'm sure it will have occurred to you. The man was actually seen only by Aileen and Ann Weston, and now that Aileen Weston is dead we are left with the uncorroborated testimony of her sister."

"Not uncorroborated surely. Mrs. Lori Weston testified that Aileen had told her that she saw this man."

Rodericks saw his opening and took it with a perfectly straight face. "I'm sorry, sir. I'm afraid I was speaking from a legal point of view. Aileen's statement to Mrs. Weston is hearsay, isn't it? You know — 'What the soldier said isn't evidence.' "

Gilbert coughed and took off his glasses. Without them his face looked much younger.

"There is that, of course. But I think for our purposes we can assume that Aileen did say she saw the man. And if she said that, thus corroborating Ann Weston's story, then we may assume that there really *was* a man."

"Not necessarily. Ann and Aileen could both have been lying. Or Ann and Mrs. Weston could both be lying now about what Aileen said."

"All right," said Gilbert a little testily. "Somebody broke the window. Somebody made the chisel marks on the window sill."

"Undoubtedly, sir. But let's look at the evidence against there ever having been such a man. Or more accurately against this man's being someone out of the blue and not a member of the Weston family or an immediate friend of the family."

"Good. Good," said Gilbert, putting his hands together on

the desk top. "This is exactly what I had hoped for. We strike sparks from each other. Go on."

"First of all, there is the fact that Aileen opened the door to him and let him into the house. She would have been unlikely to do that for a perfect stranger. They talked together in low voices — again an indication that they were acquainted. Then there is the strange business of the first phone call that afternoon after Mrs. Weston had left. From what Ann Weston says, it was certainly someone who knew the Westons well. Aileen talked about going on to the Valentine party. But who made the call? I suggest that it is possible that it was the murderer phoning to make sure that Aileen was home and that Mrs. Weston was not. Remember, there would normally have been *three* women in the house at that time in the afternoon. If it was not the murderer who placed that call, why hasn't whoever made it come forward?"

"Yes, John. I had considered that. And I agree. Your point, I take it, is that it had to be someone known to Aileen Weston and therefore not our mysterious X?"

"That's right. But again, of course, we've only got Ann's word for it that there was such a phone call."

"We are finding out — aren't we — that we've only got Ann Weston's word for quite a few things, John. Still, we must be fair. Isn't there another possibility that would account both for the phone call and for Aileen Weston admitting a stranger? Suppose someone telephoned and said something like this — 'This is Joe Doe of the hydroelectric company. Is Mrs. Weston at home? No? Well, will there be someone in the house in five minutes' time? I'd like to come around and check the meter. It won't take more than a minute.' What do you think of that?"

"I think, sir," said Rodericks, "that you are a very able lawyer and that you would be as good appearing for the defense as for the crown."

He meant it, and Gilbert sensed that he meant it, and blushed like a schoolboy.

"Do you think it likely though?"

"Frankly, no," said Rodericks. "I don't."

Gilbert sighed. "No more do I. So where does all this leave us?"

"Scratch the mysterious X."

"I'm afraid so. Yes, I'm very much afraid so. And if we rule out X, we also rule out the possibility that the wrong sister was murdered, because only a stranger could have killed the wrong girl by mistake."

"If it was done by a stranger, how can we speak of the wrong girl?" Rodericks asked. "A stranger would have killed indiscriminately. Unless you mean that there was a hired killer involved."

"I'm not suggesting that at all. Please don't try to complicate things needlessly, John." Gilbert looked at the policeman a little doubtfully. "You don't believe it *could* have been a hired killer, do you?"

"I think it highly unlikely."

"I'm glad to hear it." The crown attorney picked up the manila folder and held it about a foot above the desk top. There was drama in the gesture. "That means," he said, "that this file contains the name of a murderer."

Rodericks nodded. "Or a murderess."

"How very right you are. So let's go on to the next name on my list of suspects. Let us consider Ann Weston herself. You must have thought a good deal about that possibility. What, in your opinion, is the case against her?"

Rodericks leaned back in his chair, and began to tick off his points on his fingers. "One. Her story generally is weak. There is a vagueness about times, there are mysterious figures glimpsed in the shadows or seen dimly through the frosted glass of the front door —"

"One minute." Gilbert held up his hand. "Let me interrupt. Couldn't this very vagueness be a point in her favor? After all, it must have been a terrifying experience. Her sister murdered. She herself escaping only by running out into the snow in her stocking feet. You see what I mean?"

"I certainly do. And I agree. But I thought you wanted me to summarize the possible case against her."

"So I do. So I do. Go on."

"Two. We have only her word for two important happenings — the first telephone call and the caller at the front door. Also, as we have already discussed, we've only her word for the second occasion the mysterious follower appeared."

Gilbert bobbed his head in agreement, and Rodericks continued, "Three. She says she did not hear the second series of shots. This is not much of a point, actually. She was presumably at the foot of the garden at the time. There was a strong wind and it was blowing from her toward the house."

"But shots are loud," Gilbert protested. "Surely she would have heard them?"

"About five years ago," said Rodericks, "I was foolish

enough to get lost in the bush on a hunting trip in Northern Ontario. As night fell, I climbed the nearest piece of high ground, built myself a fire and settled down to wait for morning. About midnight I heard a jeep on a road — it turned out that the road was no more than fifty yards away — and I knew it was my friends looking for me. I fired my rifle into the air a dozen times as that jeep went back and forth so close to me, but the wind was wrong and they didn't hear a thing."

Gilbert, who was no woodsman, looked skeptical. "If you were only fifty yards from the road, why didn't you walk to it then and there?" he asked.

"I had no flashlight and it would have been far too dangerous at night. But my point was that the wind —"

"Yes. I see. All right. So it could have happened the way she said. Although, you know, all these little difficulties in her evidence do increase its improbability, don't you think? What's your fourth point?"

"Four. She had a motive. Two motives really. The money and the fact that her sister was dead set against her having anything to do with Carl Fleury."

Gilbert smiled grimly. "A hundred and seventy-five thousand dollars. Not inadequate as a motive, I'd say."

"Five," said Rodericks. "The type of wounds. I mean, of course, the first three wounds, the ones that wounded Aileen Weston, knocked her down and probably rendered her unconscious but did not kill her. One might argue that a woman or someone unused to small arms probably fired that first series of shots."

"I see from my notes that someone has already argued exactly that."

"Yes. It was one of the first things Dr. Bannister suggested to me. And Carl Fleury made the same point a little differently when he was at pains to stress his own proficiency as a pistol shot."

"Anything else?"

"Two things. Points six and seven. If, as seems probable, Dr. Weston's revolver was used for the killing, Ann Weston had ready access to that revolver. And finally there are her footprints in the snow — relatively far apart and shallow going away from the house but closer together and deeper returning."

Gilbert leaned forward eagerly. "I have the feeling, John, that this session today may not be as long as I had thought. Let's put all that you have just said together and build up a picture." He paused and placed his fingertips together. "It's a pretty ghastly picture, too.

"Here we have a girl who has been under her older sister's thumb all her life, resenting it — probably resenting it bitterly after Carl Fleury went away and joined the army. She stands to profit financially from her sister's death as well as obtaining emotional satisfaction from it. She plans her crime carefully. Somehow she gets her sister to agree that they were followed home on one occasion. Perhaps, indeed, they actually were followed that first time. That might have been what gave her the idea.

"She claims to have been followed a second time. People believe her because of the first incident. She breaks a pane of glass in the kitchen window and uses her own chisel to mark up the windowsill."

"We can't prove that," said Rodericks. "It's a strong possibility that it was the same chisel, but we can't prove it."

Gilbert waved the objection away.

"Now she has the stage set. She takes her father's revolver and when she and her sister are alone in the house — with her stepmother actually going to the police to report her mythical molester — she commits murder."

Harrison Gilbert sat back in his chair. He looked quietly proud. Rodericks had seen chess players lean back with the same expression on their faces after having made what they thought was a brilliant move.

"Apart from Mrs. Middleborough, Mrs. Weston apparently did not tell anyone that she was going to the police station that afternoon," he pointed out.

Gilbert gestured with his right hand, as a man might brush away a fly, and continued with his exposition.

"She fired three times. At the head, because she is not accustomed to firearms. Her sister screams at the first shot, but with the third shot she is hit in the temple and falls unconscious, covered with blood. Ann Weston stands over her for a moment. Perhaps she is appalled at what she has done now that the deed is actually accomplished. She walks out of the house by the back door, going slowly and fearfully, her head bowed."

"The mark of Cain upon her," said Rodericks solemnly. He could not resist saying it, but it was perhaps fortunate that Gilbert was too engrossed in his recreation of the murder to pay any heed.

"Then," said Gilbert, "then, while she is standing in the garden summoning up the necessary courage to go through with the rest of her charade — then she hears something! She hears her sister cry out! Aileen is not dead after all. Quick! She must get back to the house and finish the job —

before somebody comes, before somebody else hears, before Aileen can reach the telephone, before her father returns from work. She runs back to the house. Her sister is lying in a pool of blood by the overturned chair. Still alive. Perhaps still conscious even. Ann Weston deliberately places the revolver against her sister's breast and pulls the trigger three times!"

Gilbert took off his glasses. "Well?" he asked.

"It could be," said Rodericks. "I'll not deny it could have happened like that. As you say, a pretty ghastly possibility."

"Have we got a case?" asked Gilbert.

"No," Rodericks replied. "We have not got a case. Not yet, in any event. Let us now look at the evidence for the defense."

"All right. We must, of course. But you know, I'm almost convinced that the picture I have just painted for you is the true one."

"You certainly painted it very convincingly. But with respect, sir, there is more to be said. The strongest point against your case, in my opinion, is the fact that we have not yet been able to find the revolver. We have searched very thoroughly. The house has been gone over with a fine-tooth comb. So has the back yard and the whole area adjacent to the house. So has the Middleborough house where Ann Weston went. What could she have done with the murder weapon?"

"That's not an insoluble problem, John. For one thing — and we must hope this is what happens — it may still be found."

"But if it isn't?"

"She may have planned this long in advance, you know. Are you sure you have considered every possibility? Every place she could conceivably have hidden the gun?"

"Of course I'm not sure. How could I be? But you haven't answered my question. What if the revolver is never found?"

"She could have had an accomplice," said Gilbert. "That is the most likely answer, isn't it?"

"Who?"

"Carl Fleury, wouldn't you think? He was living right across the street. It was to that house that Ann Weston fled. Suppose he disposed of the gun?"

"If Fleury and Ann Weston were accomplices, wouldn't it be more likely that Fleury and not the girl actually committed the murder?"

"You're making difficulties, John. You're making difficulties. Fleury could have been an accessory after the fact rather than an accomplice. Suppose he was suddenly confronted by the girl he loved — by the girl he had loved for years — she tells him some story — tearfully — remorsefully. She claims, perhaps, that it was an accident, that the pistol went off by mistake —"

"Six times?"

"Damn it, John, I'm merely thinking aloud. She might have claimed it was self-defense. In any case she tells him that Aileen is dead and that she has killed her. What would Fleury do?"

"Dispose of the revolver," said Rodericks without any hesitation. "Cover up for her. Probably dispose of the body, if I'm right about that young man."

"You see?"

Rodericks shook his head. "It won't wash, sir. Where would this meeting between Ann Weston and Fleury have taken place? If it was at Mrs. Middleborough's, she would have known about it — and I'll swear she didn't. If Fleury had walked into the Weston house and found Ann standing over her murdered sister's body, he would never have let her run across the street and report it before he had tidied up and seen that she was in the clear."

Gilbert drew down the corners of his mouth. "All right. Suppose someone else took the revolver away from the scene of the crime. Suppose Ann Weston left it beside the body. The doctor — what's his name? Bannister — Dr. Bannister, an old friend of the family, who is the first to arrive — he got there ahead of the police, you will recall — suppose he disposed of the revolver? Put it in his little black bag and simply carried it away?"

"Why should he do that?"

"He recognized the revolver as Dr. Weston's. He guessed what had happened. Or it needn't have been the doctor. Or Fleury. How about Mrs. Weston as an accomplice after the fact? She finds Ann Weston beside the dead body of her sister and, anxious to save a scandal or because she loves Ann, she takes the revolver away with her. It might have been in her car when she was at the police station."

"Aren't you forgetting something, sir?" Rodericks asked. "Mrs. Weston was actually in the police station, talking to Corporal Moore and Constable Holmstead, when the murder took place."

"I never liked that bit," growled Gilbert. "It's too

damned convenient. It hasn't got the right smell. There's something fishy about that bit."

"I know what you mean, and I've wondered myself. But as far as I can see, the time of the murder is fixed by two independent witnesses. Mrs. Fitzpatrick, who in my opinion is certainly telling the truth, says she was talking to Aileen Weston at five minutes to six. Mrs. Falls heard shots at five past six. Whether it was the first series or the second, doesn't really matter, although it was probably the first. And Mrs. Lori Weston was undoubtedly at the police station from six o'clock until twenty past."

Gilbert brought his fist down on the glass top of his desk.

"We're missing something, damn it!" he said. "We have to be missing something!"

"Before we leave it, sir, there are certain other points in Ann Weston's favor."

"Are there? All right. What?"

"Nothing very definite, I'll grant you," said Rodericks. "But both the motives you have suggested seem somewhat weak. The money, for instance. It would be a much stronger motive for murder if Ann Weston were penniless and stood to gain $175,000 from her sister's death. But Ann already has $175,000 of her own. The other motive is more difficult to assess, but she is free, white and twenty-one. Presumably if she wanted to jilt Dunn and marry Carl Fleury she could have done so without committing murder first."

"Is that all?"

"No. Not quite. There is a good deal of testimony to the effect that Ann and her sister were on excellent terms, that they were genuinely fond of each other. This type of evidence can't simply be dismissed. It has to be weighed, sir."

"I know it has to be weighed, damn it, man!" said Gilbert. "I'm the lawyer. Remember? What else?"

"Only that I'm the detective with the experience, sir. Remember? And I don't think Ann Weston is a murderess. I could well be wrong. I've known a few very unlikely-looking killers in my day. Just the same, I don't think I *am* wrong. Not until some stronger evidence comes up, at all events."

"How *did* she strike you?" Gilbert asked curiously. He would never have admitted it, but he had an enormous respect for the inspector's judgment.

"A simple girl," Rodericks said. "Perhaps not overly intelligent. But a nice, simple girl. Someone who should make a good wife and mother. Her father said she was tough and I would guess he was right. Not too much imagination but plenty of what used to be called character."

Gilbert did not appear unduly disturbed at the inspector's refusal to accept his theory. "Right," he said. "If we dismiss for the moment the hypothesis that Ann Weston was the murderess, and if we likewise dismiss, again only for the moment, the hypothesis that she was an accomplice of the murderer we must accept her story as true. We have to rely upon her evidence — all of it — the molester, the first telephone call, the man who rang the doorbell and came in to kill her sister. We accept that all this happened as she said it happened. Therefore when we consider the possible cases against other suspects, we must make those cases jibe with all Ann Weston's evidence."

"Not necessarily," said Rodericks. "She could be mistaken. Or she could be lying for some other motive." Gilbert made a deprecating little gesture with his head. "But I agree we should seriously consider the possibility that Ann Weston is telling the literal truth."

"Let's take Carl Fleury next," suggested the crown attorney. "And let's try to speed this up a little. You want to get back to Farnham and I have an appointment at five. Fleury has no alibi. His motives are the same as Ann Weston's — first the money, which he would get if he married Ann, and secondly he might have been tired of Aileen's interference with his love life. He has a previous record of violence and, all in all, he sounds like a ruthless, confident type. The fact that the first three shots failed to kill the victim could have been a deliberate blind. This appears the more probable in view of the fact that Fleury was quick to point out that if he had been the killer one bullet would have been all that was needed. Anything else?"

"That sums it up, I think. But could he have got hold of the revolver? I was told that today was the first time he had set foot in the Weston house since his return. If he could have got the revolver — and I admit it shouldn't have been too hard — he had plenty of opportunity for disposing of it. Yes, the case against Fleury is not a bad one. There is just this though — I think it's only possible if Ann Weston was an accomplice. Otherwise I don't believe Fleury would have taken the chance of killing Aileen when her sister was in the house."

"Fair enough. How about Fred Dunn? He has no alibi. Since he was still engaged to Ann Weston and presumably didn't know about Fleury, he would have expected to profit from the murder. He doesn't sound like somebody who would have had much experience with firearms, and he could easily have got the revolver and disposed of it later."

"A weaker case than the one against Fleury," Rodericks suggested, "and most of the same objections apply. Would he have done it with Ann in the house? Unless they were accomplices, that is?"

"It could be that Ann Weston's affair with Fleury is so much eyewash. A cover for the real accomplice, who is Dunn."

"It's a possibility," admitted the inspector, "but I don't believe it."

"No," said Gilbert, "neither do I really. Paul Anstruthers?"

"Motive is very weak. He may have thought that Aileen had made a will in his favor. She might even have told him so. But would anyone commit murder without being sure of such an important point?"

"Would he have had any reason to disbelieve his fiancée if she had told him she had made such a will?"

It was Rodericks' turn to shrug. "He could have obtained the revolver. Also disposed of it. The type of wounds would be consistent with Anstruthers' guilt, I imagine. But that's all. Nothing to be excited about."

"Are we sure that it had to be a man?" asked the crown attorney. "The answer surely is: no, we're not. But we tend to assume that it was. If it wasn't Ann Weston, I mean. What do you have against Mrs. Middleborough?"

"Practically nothing," said Rodericks. "She is Fleury's aunt. You could argue, I suppose, that she had a motive — to see her loved nephew married to a rich girl. She had access to the weapon and opportunity to commit the crime. It's harder to see how she could have disposed of the revolver after the murder, and I can think of no reason why she should have made that first telephone call. All she would have had to do was watch by her living room window until she saw Mrs. Weston leave the house."

Gilbert made a little pencil note in his file. "Middleborough unlikely," he said. "Right. Dr. Bannister?"

"What about motive?" countered Rodericks. "Why should the doctor want to kill Aileen Weston? Apart from that, he did have the opportunity. He lives only about two blocks away from the Weston house and he could have got back there after the murder in time to take Mrs. Middleborough's phone call. He presumably had access to the revolver since he would be in and out of the Weston house in his medical capacity and as a friend of the family. He could easily have disposed of the weapon. That's all for Bannister, I think."

"Damn!" said Gilbert. "Somebody must have done it. Mrs. Weston?"

"No opportunity — unless there has been some very strange tinkering with the time of death. She was actually in the police station when the shots were fired."

"I still don't like that," said Gilbert. "She could have got the revolver, of course. She could have faked the break-in. She could have made the first telephone call. But we can't get around her alibi." He brightened a little. "She could easily be an accomplice though, couldn't she?"

"If you are going to consider Mrs. Weston as a possible suspect, you should logically also consider Constable Holmsted one." Rodericks briefly outlined Ann's story about the comic Valentine. "A weak motive, certainly, but murder has been done for less. We assume, of course, that Holmsted actually did see Aileen Weston in the bookshop and was afraid she would snitch on him."

"Nonsense," said Gilbert, brightening even more as he saw a chance to score off the inspector. "Absolute nonsense. In that case, he simply wouldn't have sent the Valentine."

Rodericks grinned. "Very well. *Touché*. But it could have happened differently. Say he had already sent the Valentine and then the shop-girl told him that Aileen had seen him buy it."

"I am getting damned tired of all this supposition," declared Gilbert. "Let's call it a day, shall we? Have we missed anyone?"

"Dr. Weston."

"That's absurd. There is such a thing, John, as being too thorough. Why on earth should Weston kill his own daughter?"

"Supposing she wasn't his daughter? Supposing Weston's whole story about Lori is really the truth turned inside out — that it was the first Mrs. Weston who was unfaithful? The Rebecca motif. He hated his first wife and he hated his first wife's child. Now Ann Weston is undoubtedly Dr. Weston's daughter. The resemblance is unmistakable. Would he have committed murder so that his own child would inherit all the money?"

"This gets more and more fantastic," said Gilbert. Then more slowly, "Of course, he could have come home earlier than he said. He had access to the murder weapon and a chance to dispose of it. Could he have faked his heart attack?"

"I very much doubt it. Dr. Bannister doesn't seem to be the kind of man who would be easily fooled. Although I have heard that if you chew a little cordite —"

Gilbert shut the folder and stood up. "Go away, John. I had hoped that this session would clarify things. All it has done is muddy the waters."

Rodericks walked across acres of carpet to the door. At the door he turned. "How about Castle?" he asked. "Could he have been embezzling the trust fund? And have been afraid it would be discovered in April when Aileen got married?"

He shut the door softly behind him, but as he walked down the corridor he could hear Gilbert swearing.

At first Rodericks was smiling to himself but as he approached the elevator his smile faded and his steps got slower and slower. He pushed the button absentmindedly and stood deep in thought until the car stopped at the seventeenth floor. When the elevator doors opened he hesitated, then turned away and strode back to Gilbert's office.

He put his head in the door. "There is one more thing," he said. The crown attorney was about to curse him for carrying a joke too far but the look on his face stopped him.

Rodericks came in and shut the door. He walked across to Gilbert's desk.

"It never struck me as strange before, but as I walked out of here just now I suddenly thought —"

"Well, out with it, man! What did you think?"

"Have you got that list of suspects handy? Let's have a

look at it. Now — see where we've listed motives. This is what I mean —"

Rodericks spoke earnestly for about a minute and Gilbert listened without interrupting. When the inspector had finished a little silence fell. At last Gilbert said, "I am persuaded. But what do we do now?"

"I'm getting back to Farnham as fast as I can," said Rodericks. "Please God I'll be in time. Would you telephone Peele and warn him? Tell him to search Ann Weston's room thoroughly and not to leave her alone for a minute. If she goes to her bedroom, have him put a guard on the door."

Gilbert was already picking up the phone when Rodericks left.

13

It was a quarter past five and the sun was setting when Rodericks got out of the police cruiser in front of the Weston house. The sky over Farnham was clear and the world seemed filled with a faint crimson light that reflected off the snow and shone blankly from all the windowpanes that faced the west. Above the intervening rooftops the square brick tower of St. John's Anglican Church on Main Street looked as though it had been blacked in with India ink. Seen thus in outline, it appeared authentically Norman, as though it had been built in 1113 instead of 1913.

Rodericks reflected that at this time yesterday it had been as dark as night, with the setting sun hidden by high-piled storm clouds. And at this time yesterday Aileen Weston had still been alive. There had been three women in this house, getting ready to go to a Valentine party. Less than twenty-four hours ago this old mansion had seemed in no way sinister, but now it was marked for the rest of its days. Until the wreckers finally demolished it, it would be a showpiece for curious strangers, "the Weston house where the murder was committed." As he climbed the verandah steps, Rodericks hoped this would be the last time he had to do so.

After the comings and goings of the previous night and this morning the house seemed quiet and almost deserted. He found Sergeant Peele in the drawing room, standing with his back to a nicely blazing log fire.

"Mrs. Weston lit it for me," he explained, "and it seemed a pity not to make the most of it."

"Very thoughtful of her. Where is she now?"

"Upstairs in her room. So is Ann Weston. Holmsted is sitting outside in the hallway. He and I are the only ones left. Moore had to go back to the office and the mine-detector crews left after lunch."

"That should be all right," said Rodericks. "We should be able to get cleaned up here this evening."

Peele's head came up. "You've got a warrant?"

"No. No warrant. But I expect to make an arrest. Is anyone else in the house?"

"Dunn's in the guest room, I think. He wanted to get in to see Miss Weston and was a bit upset when he was told he couldn't."

Rodericks smiled. "Is she all right?"

"Not really. She's still inclined to be weepy and hysterical. She wanted to go to the hospital to see her father but Dr. Bannister talked her out of that. He said it would be too hard on both of them, and he told me that he would have hospitalized her himself if he could have got a bed. But he couldn't, so he put her to bed here."

"You searched her room before she was put to bed, did you?"

"Corporal Moore did. I stayed downstairs with her while he was at it. Nothing was found. I looked in on her half an hour ago and she cowered back as though I was the devil come to get her."

"I think I'll take a look at her myself," Rodericks decided. "Her room's the second on the right at the top of the stairs, isn't it?"

He went up the stairs quickly, taking them two at a time. Constable Holmsted sat on a kitchen chair halfway down the hall. The inspector waved for him to remain where he was. He knocked on the door of Ann's room, opened it and looked in. Ann, clad in a red housecoat, was sitting bolt upright in her bed, a frightened look on her face.

"Are you all right, Miss Weston?" Rodericks' eyes made a quick survey of the room, missing nothing. "You should be resting."

"I'm fine, Inspector," Ann replied in a shaky voice. Then as an afterthought. "Thank you."

There was a grim little smile on Rodericks' face as he went downstairs. Peele was still standing by the fire.

"Where are the others?" Rodericks asked.

"Dr. Bannister is at the hospital. I understand that Weston has taken a turn for the worse, by the way. Carl Fleury is across the street at his aunt's, as far as I know. Anstruthers said he was going down to the hotel for a drink."

"Get them all back here, Ted, will you? As soon as possible. I want to get this over with. Better have Moore come in, too. We'll use this room."

As Peele moved away, Lori Weston came down the stairs. She smiled at Peele, who checked his stride as though he had been hit, but she went past him and approached the inspector.

She was as lovely and as fragrant as ever, but Rodericks, scrutinizing her closely, thought she had been crying. She looked up at him, her face serious.

"I heard what you said just now — about getting it over with. Does that mean you are going to arrest Ann?"

"Mrs. Weston, why are you so sure that Ann is the one who is guilty?"

"I am not sure of anything of the sort. I am sure she is *not* guilty. And I have no doubt at all that she will be able to prove it. But, Inspector, perhaps you haven't heard — Bob — my husband — had another heart attack this afternoon. His condition is very critical. If he heard that Ann had been arrested it would kill him."

"There is no reason why he should hear of it," said Rodericks.

Lori looked suddenly stricken. Her face crumpled and she half turned away. "You don't know Farnham," she said. "It's a small town. You can't keep news like that quiet, even in a hospital. He would be bound to find out." She turned back to face him. "And it will kill him, I tell you! It will kill him!"

"Mrs. Weston," said Rodericks softly, "I have not said I intend to arrest your stepdaughter. And I am sorry to hear that your husband's condition has worsened."

"Inspector Rodericks, I tell you that if you arrest Ann, you will not only be arresting an innocent girl and letting the real murderer go free, you will also be no better than a murderer yourself."

She spoke quietly but with great intensity and her attention had been wholly fixed on the inspector. Therefore she had not heard Fred Dunn come down the stairs behind her. Rodericks had watched him approach but had given no sign.

"I hear we're getting the whole cast on stage for the last act," Dunn said from immediately behind Lori. She gave a startled cry and swung around, her hand to her mouth.

"I thought it was only done in books," Dunn went on. "*The Corpse in the Library* or *The Clue of the Twisted Candle*. And if Lori's right, we're in for an extra treat. Are you getting us all together so that you can confess, Inspector?"

Lori looked at Dunn as though she could not believe he was real. She walked quickly away and took a chair in the far corner of the room. Rodericks regarded Dunn without affection.

"Sit down," he said coldly, "and be quiet. You may get a chance to speak later on." He continued to stand where he was, soaking up the heat from the fire, until Peele returned.

"Moore is on his way over, and so is Anstruthers. But I had no luck with the other two. Dr. Bannister is busy at the hospital and I couldn't speak to him. I left a message though. The nurse thought he might be available in about half an hour. Carl Fleury is nowhere to be found. Mrs. Middleborough said he was in his room but when she went to look he had gone."

"We'll wait a few minutes then," said Rodericks calmly. "Is Miss Weston not coming down?"

"I looked in on her," Peele replied. "She was sound asleep. I thought there would be no harm in letting her rest until the others showed up."

Rodericks did not seem too well pleased at this but Peele

construed his noncommittal grunt as assent. A few minutes later Corporal Moore came in, followed shortly afterward by Paul Anstruthers. Moore sat next to Lori Weston and Anstruthers took a chair beside Dunn. Rodericks looked at his watch and frowned. He was about to speak when the front door slammed. A moment later Mrs. Middleborough walked into the room. She was wearing an old blue coat over a housedress and her hair was in curlers. There was an eager expression on her face.

"I hope I'm not intruding, Inspector," she said. "I just wanted to tell you that Carl hasn't come back yet." She had the grace to blush at the transparency of this excuse but went on doggedly. "I can't think where he's got to. He hasn't come over here, has he?" Her black eyes darted inquisitively from face to face.

"Now that you're here, Mrs. Middleborough, you may as well stay," Rodericks said, ignoring her question. "You may be able to add something to the proceedings."

The invitation had been unnecessary, for Mrs. Middleborough had already seated herself firmly on the davenport and was looking as though nothing short of brute force would move her.

"We won't wait for the late arrivals, I think," the inspector went on. "Dr. Bannister should be here presently and I wouldn't be surprised if Sergeant Fleury didn't show up as well." Peele caught his eye. "No, Ted, we won't wake Miss Weston just yet. I'll ask you to do that in a few minutes."

He looked around to make sure that he held everyone's attention. The room was very quiet. Only the log fire behind him whispered gutturally in the silence.

"The crown attorney and I spent this afternoon reviewing the case," Rodericks began. "I don't intend to recapitulate it all now, but there are certain salient facts I want to bring to your attention. If any of you feel called upon to interrupt me, or to correct me on a point of fact, feel free to do so.

"As Mr. Dunn has already suggested, this method of interviewing witnesses is used more in fiction than real life. On this occasion, however, real life is going to imitate fiction. It is a phenomenon not as uncommon as you might think, and I have my reasons. They will doubtless become clear to you as I go along."

Corporal Moore's honest red face wore a puzzled frown. Mrs. Middleborough was breathing heavily and leaning forward to listen. Anstruthers and Dunn sat side by side, supercilious but somewhat apprehensive. Lori Weston was very pale and looked as though she was in pain.

"I'll start at the beginning," Rodericks said, "but I'll be as brief as I can. This case began eight days ago, on Thursday, the ninth of February. That was the day Carl Fleury arrived back in Farnham from Germany. It was also the night that Aileen and Ann Weston returned to this house with the story that they had been followed home by a mysterious stranger. Three nights later much the same thing happened, but to Ann Weston alone. On the night before the murder, according to Mrs. Weston, there was a rather clumsy attempt made to break in through the kitchen window.

"These three incidents had a single purpose behind them — they were intended to draw attention to an unknown man who was displaying a sinister interest in the Weston girls.

Yesterday afternoon Mrs. Weston reported the matter to the police. And at the very time when Mrs. Weston was in the police station, talking to two police officers, her stepdaughter, Aileen Weston, was murdered in this room."

Rodericks paused and looked to his right at the spot where Aileen's body had lain. The smudged chalk outline drawn by Dr. McCabe was still clearly visible on the hardwood floor. Everyone followed the inspector's glance. Lori Weston shivered as though from a sudden chill.

"You are all familiar with the version of subsequent events told by Ann Weston. It appeared to me that there were certain weak points in Miss Weston's story and I soon got the impression that those who were closest to her shared my feeling. Both her stepmother and Dr. Bannister, who is an old friend of the family, did their best to keep me from interviewing Miss Weston after the murder. In fact, I was unable to speak to this important witness until this morning."

Lori's clear voice broke in from the corner of the room. "That is grossly unfair, Inspector, and you know it. Ann was in no condition to be interrogated last night."

"Your objection is noted, Mrs. Weston," Rodericks replied, "but I fear you have not been listening sufficiently closely to what I have been saying. I have not questioned the genuineness of Miss Weston's nervous collapse after the murder. Indeed, I may as well state quite plainly now that I believe Ann Weston's story to be true in every particular. Let me emphasize that last point again — in every particular."

His eyes went around the room, searching each face in

turn. It took perhaps thirty seconds, during which time the tension in the room palpably increased. At last he continued, "You will remember that Ann told how she heard the shots, her sister's scream, and the thud of her sister's body falling. Then she heard the murderer's footsteps coming up those stairs." He half turned and pointed. "She ran out of the house and escaped.

"Let me emphasize that — she escaped." Again he paused for effect. "In other words, the murderer's task was only half completed, for it had been his intention from the very beginning to kill *both* girls.

"This idea, of course, was always implicit in Ann Weston's account. Remember that the murderer knew at the time he killed Aileen that Ann was in the house. If, as seems certain, it was the murderer who telephoned just before six o'clock and talked to Aileen, then he knew before he entered the house that both girls were inside — and that Mrs. Weston was not."

Rodericks stopped and looked at Lori. She returned his gaze, pale but clear-eyed. The inspector twinkled at her but there was definitely no mirth in the twinkle.

"Mrs. Weston was not," he repeated. "At that time Mrs. Weston was very conveniently at the police station. We know almost exactly how long she was there, for she arrived just as Constable Holmsted was coming on duty at six o'clock, and as she was going out of the corporal's office she drew attention to the time by looking at the clock on the wall, comparing it with her wristwatch and remarking that Mrs. Fitzpatrick would be waiting for her."

Lori half rose from her chair, her hollow cheeks drained of

color, but she sank back again without speaking. There was a look of utter incredulity on her beautiful face. Rodericks' voice took on a new note as he began to speak again. It was deeper and grimmer and had an inexorable tone to it.

"I would like you now to consider, not what actually happened yesterday evening in this house, but what was intended to happen. The murder, you see, was bungled, and bungled rather badly. First of all, Aileen was not killed outright as the killer had supposed. This, by itself, is an interesting point. The first three shots were fired at close range — probably when Aileen Weston was sitting in a chair facing her killer. Yet, despite the fact that they were fired from not more than a few feet away, none of them proved fatal. While Ann Weston was fleeing for her life in her stocking feet — along the upstairs hall, down the back stairs, out through the kitchen and into the dark garden — while Ann was doing this, as silently and as quickly as she could, her sister, lying on the floor and horribly wounded, regained consciousness. She probably cried out. Certainly she shifted her position, moving forward along the floor so that the lower part of her body covered the pool of blood where her head had been. The killer heard this movement or her cry. In any event the pursuit of Ann Weston had to be abandoned, for Aileen had to be silenced immediately. After all, only two minutes previously Aileen and the intruder had been face to face — *so Aileen knew who the intruder was.*"

Once more the twinkling gray eyes searched each face in the room in turn as though trying to read whatever secrets were being concealed. No one moved or spoke but each of the six listeners stared back fixedly.

"That was what actually happened," Rodericks went on. "What was intended was rather different. The killer had intended to shoot down Aileen Weston in this room, using not more than three of the six shots in the revolver. Then when Ann Weston came running downstairs to see what had happened, or while she remained transfixed with fright upstairs, the killer intended to use the other three shots on her. Aileen's scream ruined that plan and probably so shocked the killer that the next two shots failed to do what they had been supposed to do.

"Consider now, however, what would have happened in Farnham last night if the killer's plan had not been partially spoiled — that is, if both Aileen and Ann had been murdered. The next thing to have happened would have been for Dr. Weston to return home. His train arrived at the station at 6:05, and last night he had arranged to take a taxi because his wife and daughters would already have gone on to Mrs. Fitzpatrick's party. The train was fifteen minutes late yesterday because of the storm, but this would have made no difference to the killer's plan. Dr. Weston would have come into his house and found both his daughters murdered, lying in their own blood. Something very much like this actually occurred in any case — and Dr. Weston, as you know, immediately suffered a severe heart attack. But if the killer's plan had worked, I think that the telephone wires would have been torn out and there would certainly have been no Dr. Bannister at hand to render first aid. Bannister only arrived on the scene because Ann Weston escaped. And if Bannister had not been there within a few seconds of Dr. Weston's seizure, Weston would quite certainly have died.

As it was, it was touch and go all night long at the hospital."

Rodericks half turned so that he was looking directly at Lori. "This was the third death that had been planned and it was integral to the killer's scheme. This was the way the events of last night were supposed to happen.

"Once we understand that, certain other facts become immediately clear. When it was a question of the murder of Aileen Weston alone, the possible motives for the killing were obscure. As far as we could discover, none of the usual emotional reasons for murder were present, or not in sufficient strength. Profit is by far the commonest reason for killing. Now in the case of Aileen's death there was a considerable sum of money involved as an inheritance, but Ann Weston was the sole legatee. Financially, therefore, the murder of Aileen Weston profited only her sister — or, conceivably, either Mr. Dunn or Sergeant Fleury, both of whom wished to marry her. Mr. Anstruthers, in fact, had no motive, for even if Aileen Weston had made a will in his favor, which she did not, that will would not have affected her inheritance from the trust fund, for Aileen would not come into her inheritance until her twenty-fifth birthday or the day of her marriage, whichever was earlier. Thus, at the time of her death, Aileen Weston had no money to leave to anyone.

"When we consider the case of both girls being dead, however, and when we add to that the subsequent death of their father, the situation, financially, is at once clearer. If the two girls had both died before their father, Dr. Weston would have been the legal heir, and then when he died, Lori Weston, as the widow of Dr. Weston, would have inherited the entire estate."

Lori lurched to her feet and gave a little bleating cry. Her hands fluttered in front of her as though she was blind. Her mouth worked but she articulated no words. Watching her, Rodericks' heart almost misgave him for the pity of it.

At that instant, when everyone was watching Lori, there came a shout from the stairs. Rodericks swung around and saw Carl Fleury standing with his feet wide apart halfway down the curving staircase. He was glaring down into the drawing room with a look of terrifying ferocity on his dark face, and in his arms, her head lolling back and her eyes closed, was the limp body of Ann Weston. Hovering helplessly behind Fleury, and wearing an expression of startled idiocy, was Constable Holmsted.

Fleury walked down the remaining stairs and crossed the drawing room to stand in front of Rodericks.

"She's dead," he said. "She died within the last three minutes. I couldn't wake her and then her breathing stopped. There's no pulse."

He carried Ann over to the davenport and Mrs. Middleborough hurriedly made way for him. Gently he lowered the girl's body and then straightened.

"She's dead," he said again. "And I swear to God I'll kill whoever did it."

14

Rodericks lifted Ann Weston's left eyelid. The pupil was enormous, covering almost the entire iris. She did not seem to be breathing but the inspector could not believe that she was dead. Her symptoms were those of barbiturate poisoning and no barbiturate that Rodericks knew of could kill as quickly as that. He felt for her pulse and sure enough found it, very feeble and slow but there.

He turned about and found Lori standing beside him.

"She's alive," he said. "Get me some mustard and warm water."

Lori was halfway to the kitchen before he finished speaking and was back almost at once with a tumbler of yellowish liquid. Sergeant Peele came back from the hall.

"I still couldn't reach Bannister at the hospital," he said, "but Dr. Saunders will be over almost immediately. He said to go on doing what we're doing, and if she regains consciousness to get her on her feet and walk her about."

It was at about this time that Rodericks began to notice a strange thing. He had lost command. It was Lori Weston who forced the strong emetic down Ann's throat and who held the basins afterward, while Anstruthers and Dunn turned away with green faces. It was Lori who ordered Mrs. Middleborough to make strong black coffee. It was Lori who nursed the first flickering signs of returning consciousness and who smiled reassuringly at Ann as she opened her eyes. It was Lori who brought the heavy blanket, warmed it before the fire, and draped it across Ann's shoulders as she walked up and down the room between Fleury and Rodericks.

Once he was certain that Ann was going to survive, Fleury seemed to feel like talking.

"I was up in her room," he told the inspector, speaking across Ann, "ever since a quarter past four this afternoon. Your constable was down in the kitchen getting a cup of coffee and I went up the front stairs and walked right in. What I mean is, if I could do it, anybody could do it."

Rodericks thought about Constable Holmsted for a little space of time, but he did not confide his thoughts to the soldier.

"I was worried about her," Fleury went on. "I reasoned that someone had tried to kill her once and that they might again. I also reasoned that the police would be too busy trying to pin the murder on her to think of anything else. And I was almost right, wasn't I?"

"No," said Rodericks heavily. "I calculated it that way too. But I never considered poison."

"The stuff must have been in her Coke. She had half a bottle by her bedside. It was after she drank it that she began to get sleepy."

"Probably. We've got the Coke bottle and there is enough left in it to analyze, so we'll know for sure."

"You nearly caught me when you looked in," Fleury

said. "A good job for Ann, you didn't. She would have been dead by now. I hid in the clothes closet."

"I know," said Rodericks, and Fleury stared at him. "I heard the cupboard door shut, and Ann isn't the best actress in the world. The police haven't shown up too well this evening, as you have not hesitated to tell me, but I was quite content to leave you in Ann's room. It was an extra safeguard and I couldn't very well put a constable in with her."

"But how did you know it was me?"

"Who else? Ann wasn't screaming the house down. It had to be you."

Fleury stopped and Ann slumped against him.

"Keep walking," Rodericks said. Fleury moved off again.

"Does this mean that you don't believe Ann is guilty?"

"We're away past that," the inspector assured him. "You miss a lot if you hide yourself away."

Corporal Moore came up and walked along with them. He had a .32 caliber revolver in his hand, held carefully with thumb and forefinger on the serrated butt plates that would not take fingerprints.

"This was in the drawer of Miss Weston's bedside table," he said. "It's been fired recently."

"Yes," said Rodericks absently. "I'm not surprised. Have it fingerprinted and sent to the lab. It's the weapon that killed Aileen Weston."

"Ann never used that pistol in her life," Fleury declared heatedly. "Tell him, Ann."

"I'd like to go back to sleep please," said Ann. "I'm very sleepy."

"Keep walking," said Fleury, sounding just like the inspector.

Dr. Saunders arrived, flurried at being late. He left a trail of snow on the rug from his overshoes. He was a stout young man and he was breathing heavily as though he had been running. He looked Ann over carefully, tested her reflexes, took her pulse, listened to her breathing with a stethoscope.

"She'll be all right," he declared. "You're sure you got everything up? Hm, yes, I see you probably did. You'll be wanting this stuff for your pathologist, I suppose. Well, keep her warm and don't let her go back to sleep for an hour or two." He lowered his voice and spoke in Rodericks' ear. "Did she do it herself?"

Rodericks shook his head. "No. It was given to her."

"That's all right then. You'll see she isn't given any more of whatever it was. I'd put her in the hospital if I could, but I can't. We've got cots in the corridors. Got to run now, but George Bannister will be along soon. Anyway she's going to be all right."

Dr. Saunders departed in a rush, his overcoat unbuttoned and his scarf trailing behind him. Corporal Moore removed the basins and Lori did some tidying by the davenport. Ann, still protesting feebly, was made to walk some more, although now she was able to get along with only Fleury for support. They strolled carefully through the French doors and into the back parlor. Rodericks looked after them, noticing the dark head nestled on Fleury's shoulder and the khaki-clad arm around Ann's waist. Like a scene from *Smiling Through,* he thought to himself.

A few minutes later Dr. Bannister came in. He looked ill and deadly tired. Lori went up to him at once.

"How is he?"

Bannister shook his head gravely and took her hand.

"He's still alive, Lori, but I'm afraid I can hold out no hope. He is not in any pain."

Lori turned away and Rodericks saw that the tears were streaming down her face.

Dr. Bannister approached him.

"I don't see Ann here," he said. "I think I had better go to her. She should be told about her father."

"How long is he likely to last?" Rodericks asked.

The doctor gave a weary little shrug. "It's impossible to say. He has had a new series of heart attacks this afternoon and massive damage has been done. He may last a few days more, but I'm afraid it's more likely he'll slip away in the early hours of the morning. Is Ann still in her room?"

"No, Miss Weston has had a narrow escape from death, but she is now recovering nicely."

"An escape from death?" Bannister's face, pale before, lost every vestige of color. "She's all right?"

"Yes, she's all right now, but it was a near thing for a few minutes. She was poisoned."

Bannister collapsed into an armchair as though his legs could no longer support him. "My God!" he said. "My God!"

Fleury and Ann came back through the French doors and sat down on the davenport. Bannister got to his feet and went over to them. He questioned Ann urgently and seemed to be reassured by her replies. Tentatively Fleury took his arm away from her shoulders and when she seemed able to sit up without his support he went across to the inspector.

"She's afraid to go back to her room. I'm going to take her across to my house tonight. Aunt Bess can look after her. May we go now?"

"I would rather you waited a few minutes more, if you would. I won't take long."

"All right," said Fleury. "But she's had a hell of a day. A hell of a time for the last twenty-four hours. She needs care."

"You'll see that she gets it," Rodericks replied with a smile. "There's nothing more to worry about now. Will you be taking her back to Germany?"

"As soon as I can," Fleury said grimly. He went back to Ann and sat down beside her.

Rodericks raised his voice. "Would you all pay attention, please. I won't keep you long."

Lori stepped toward him.

"Isn't it about over?" she asked. "I'd like to pack a few things to take with me. And I want to call a lawyer. Not Mr. Castle, I think."

She had recovered her composure, but she seemed drained of all her vitality. For the first time she looked her age or perhaps a little more, but she was still very lovely. She turned and began to walk toward the stairs.

"Do you want to send someone with me?" Over her shoulder her eyes rested on Sergeant Peele. He started forward as though drawn on a string.

"Sit down, Mrs. Weston," said Rodericks. "You are not under arrest. All of you sit down."

It took them a moment or two to sort themselves out and form a half-circle around the inspector. Corporal Moore and Constable Holmsted stood in the background near the door to the hall. Sergeant Peele lounged against the French doors into the back parlor. Anstruthers and Dunn pulled up chairs and sat close together on Rodericks' left. Next to them was Mrs. Middleborough and then Lori and Dr. Bannister. Carl Fleury and Ann remained together on the davenport.

"I intend to take up again from the point I had reached when I was interrupted," Rodericks said. "You will remember that I had outlined the case for Mrs. Weston being the murderess. I had been about to observe, however, that this case seemed to be contradicted by a fact that has troubled me all along. I mean, of course, that Mrs. Weston was actually at the police station when the murder was committed.

"I said that this fact troubled me. It did so because it seemed to me altogether too good an alibi. We are able to fix the time of the murder as between six and twenty past six. The estimate of time rested primarily on Miss Weston's testimony, but Miss Weston was supported by two other witnesses on this point. Mrs. Fitzpatrick said that she had been talking on the telephone to Aileen Weston at six o'clock or one or two minutes before six. Therefore the dead girl was not killed until after that time. Mrs. Falls, who happened to be passing by on the street outside, heard three shots at five minutes past six. Dr. Bannister, who was first on the scene after Ann Weston had fled across the street, found Aileen dead at six-twenty or six-twenty-one. Corporal Moore and Constable Holmsted arrived a minute or two later.

"With this evidence it was impossible to believe that the murder had been committed either earlier or later than our estimate. There was, of course, the possibility that Mrs. Fitzpatrick had been mistaken in believing that it had been Aileen she had been talking to on the telephone — a most unlikely mistake, for Mrs. Fitzpatrick knew Aileen's voice well. This explanation would also have had to mean that Ann Weston was lying about the time of the murder, and, moreover, that she was lying to give her stepmother an alibi. Accordingly, I dismissed this hypothesis as too improbable to merit further consideration.

"There was, however, still another possibility to be considered. Was it possible that there was an error in the report that Mrs. Weston had been in the police station between six and twenty past? Corporal Moore and Constable Holmsted both testified that she was. She had arrived just after Holmsted came on duty and before she left she had drawn attention to the time, looking at the clock on the wall and saying that she would be late for Mrs. Fitzpatrick's party. Corporal Moore verified the time by looking at his own watch. Therefore Mrs. Weston was undoubtedly where she said she was and thus could not conceivably have murdered Aileen Weston.

"Her motive nevertheless looked as strong as ever. There was a sum of approximately $350,000 at stake and I was convinced that this was somehow the reason for the crime. Was it possible, I asked myself, that Mrs. Weston had an accomplice? Someone who actually committed the murder for her while she was providing herself with the perfect alibi? It seemed more than possible. It seemed extremely likely. And this was a discouraging thought, for I realize that if this was the case the guilty parties stood an excellent chance of getting clean away with it. Mrs. Weston's accomplice could be anyone, even a hired killer.

"One small fact, however, led me to question the truth of this hypothesis. If an accomplice of Mrs. Weston's had killed Aileen, what had been the purpose of the first telephone call that Aileen took at five to six? No one had admitted making such a call and it seemed probable that it had been made by the murderer, who had wanted to be sure that the two girls were in the house alone. If the murderer had conspired with Mrs. Weston, no such call would have been necessary for he would have known what she intended to do and when she would do it. If any liaison had been required, it would have been simpler and more natural for Mrs. Weston to have telephoned her accomplice immediately before she left the house, saying, in effect, 'All right. The coast is clear. Come and do it now.' "

The telephone rang in the hall and Corporal Moore slipped out to answer it. Rodericks went on, "There were also other things which made me disinclined to believe in Mrs. Weston's guilt. Not least of them was her character as attested to by everyone who knew her. My own observation tended to confirm that Mrs. Weston had a sweet and amiable disposition and that violence of any sort was repugnant to her. 'No one can quarrel with Lori,' her husband said, and her neighbors and friends all confirmed this judgment. My experience has been that character evidence is generally quite reliable. Murder is not a freakish accident that can crop up in anyone's life. It has deep roots that have grown slowly over a long period of time. And that has been true in this case as well."

Corporal Moore came back into the drawing room. He had a folded slip of paper in his hand which he passed to the inspector. Rodericks read it and put it in his pocket.

"In this case," Rodericks went on, "we are confronted

with a murderer who had planned the death, not of one, but of three people in order to gain his end. I asked myself why he should not have contemplated four deaths instead of three. The fourth death, of course, being Mrs. Weston's. In such a chain of calamity, the tax gatherer would have taken a sizable portion of the $350,000 in death duties, but there would still have been a very worthwhile sum left to be inherited.

"Who then would Mrs. Weston's heirs have been if her stepdaughters and husband had both predeceased her? Here again it looked as though I had strayed up a cul de sac, for Mrs. Weston was an orphan who had no living relatives. Or none of which she knew. Moreover, Mrs. Weston is — as I am sure you will all agree — a woman of outstanding beauty and charm. If our murderer was to inherit from her, he would not be able to wait too long before he struck again, for the chances would be good that Mrs. Weston would remarry."

Rodericks paused and looked about him. Lori was white and shaking and there was a growing look of horror in her lovely green eyes.

"Remarry," Rodericks repeated. "That was the key I had been seeking. Who was there who could be reasonably sure that he could marry Mrs. Weston if her husband died? This should have occurred to me sooner, for I had been told that all was not well with Mrs. Weston's marriage."

Lori stared at him with a look of amazement. "You were told *what?*"

"That you had a lover."

Rodericks did not consider his statement to be untrue. If

he had been accused of deception, he would have replied that people communicated with one another by several different mediums, that Dr. Weston had told him, in everything but so many words, that he believed his wife to be unfaithful to him.

Lori's beautiful face twisted with grief but Rodericks could detect no shadow of fear in her expression. She said quite simply, "Bob and I love one another." She looked past him, her green eyes misty, a queen out of some old romance, ensnared by dark enchantments whose spell she could not break. "Life is not always as uncomplicated as you seem to think, Inspector."

"What do you mean by that?"

"What I say. And I see no need to discuss my private life with the police."

Rodericks stared at her for a moment, then continued, speaking to the room at large.

"It had to be a man who was well known to Aileen Weston, for she had admitted him without question to the house and had talked to him familiarly on the telephone. It had to be someone who had access to Dr. Weston's revolver, and, as we now know, it had to be someone who had access to a fatal dosage of some barbiturate. The choice of that particular method to kill Ann Weston was an act of desperation. But then time was desperately short, for Dr. Weston might die at any moment. And if he died as much as two minutes before his daughter, Mrs. Weston would never touch the trust fund. No wonder you worked so hard to keep your patient alive, Dr. Bannister."

Bannister was on his feet, his face working. Corporal

Moore and Sergeant Peele moved up to stand behind him. Rodericks' voice went on inexorably, "You have always had a good deal of success with women, haven't you, Dr. Bannister? Perhaps we shall find that that was one of the reasons why a physician as competent as yourself decided to leave the city and accept an obscure practice in a small town. Certainly every single woman who has been in any way connected with this case has been susceptible to your charm. Every one of them has had something good to say about you. Not that that told against you, of course. Quite the contrary, but it is really not surprising that Mrs. Weston, married to a man fifteen years older than herself, should have allowed herself to become fond of you."

Lori had buried her face in her hands and when Rodericks spoke to her his voice became gentle.

"I am sorry to have to confront you in this way, Mrs. Weston. And I apologize for having given you a bad few minutes earlier this evening, but I was afraid that a mistaken sense of loyalty to Bannister might lead you to deny your relationship with him. After the attempt on Ann's life, I do not think that likely."

Lori looked up at that. Rodericks thought that he detected a new resolution in her face.

"I knew, of course, that you had been friendly with Bannister before you married Dr. Weston, for you inadvertently told me so yourself. You said you had known him for ten years. Bannister, however, had been at pains to tell me that he had met you only after your marriage. Of the two statements, yours and Bannister's, I preferred to believe yours on general principles. Certainly there are more obvious reasons for the denial of a real male-female relationship than for the invention of a fictitious one. At the time I did not understand the other half of what you said. I think your exact words were — 'but I never realized how devoted a doctor he was until tonight.' Properly understood, that was a most revealing comment. Bannister, after all, had done only what any good doctor would have done — worked hard to save the life of a patient. But you were particularly impressed with his devotion to his profession because you knew that he wanted to marry you and that you would not consent to that while your husband was alive. That's right, isn't it?"

"Yes," said Lori. "That's right." It seemed to Rodericks that the fatality he had previously sensed in her had become more explicit. Perhaps Helen had worn just such a look as she had watched tall Troy burning, knowing that it had all been done for her. Lori spoke again and there was a note of wondering sadness in her voice, "I told you life was complicated. It is possible to love two people, Inspector, in different ways. At least it is possible for me."

"Thank you, Mrs. Weston." To get it on the record, he asked, "You and Bannister have been lovers for how long?"

Lori's reply was low but distinct. "About eight months."

"Lori, you don't have to say anything," Bannister exclaimed. "This is all a tissue of lies! Please don't go along with it."

Rodericks turned back to the doctor and his voice hardened again. "You were not cut out to be a murderer, Bannister. You have made almost every mistake it was possible for you to make."

"I deny this preposterous charge," Bannister said. "You'll never prove it."

"We will. We will prove your previous association with

Mrs. Weston and we will prove that that relationship was resumed here in Farnham eight months ago."

"There is no law against that," said Bannister.

"I said that as a murderer you were a bungler, Doctor. Do you know that Ann Weston's room was searched this afternoon at four o'clock before she was allowed to retire there with a police guard outside her door? There was no revolver in the room then. You placed it there when you went in to visit her as her physician after you had ordered her to bed. And you dropped the poison in the Coke bottle at the same time. Miss Weston, did he try to give you a sedative at that time?"

Ann held Fleury's hand tightly in her own. "Yes. Yes, he did. I told him I wouldn't take anything to put me to sleep. I wanted to be awake, because —"

"Because you knew Carl was coming. Exactly. Now, Miss Weston, I have one more question. Were you ever alone between the time I telephoned from London at three-thirty this afternoon and now — apart from the time you were alone in your own room?"

Ann thought back. "No," she said at last. "Sergeant Peele was with me all the time."

"I should hope so," said Rodericks. "He was told not to let you out of his sight. And now, Constable Holmsted, how many people went into Miss Weston's bedroom this afternoon?"

"Only Dr. Bannister, sir. He went in at a little after four o'clock and stayed for about five minutes."

Carl Fleury opened his mouth to speak but Rodericks gave him a look and he subsided.

"Her room was searched at four o'clock, Bannister. No revolver was there then. And no one but you entered the room after that. It had to be you who brought it in."

"No." Bannister's voice was hoarse and his eyes were wild. "It's a lie! She must have concealed it somewhere. You must have missed it. She killed her sister and then tried to commit suicide."

"Well," said Rodericks, "we will certainly find Miss Weston's fingerprints on the revolver. I'm sure of that."

"You see! Then why are you accusing me?"

"Because I am sure you placed Miss Weston's fingerprints on the pistol last night when she was in a drugged sleep at Mrs. Middleborough's. Your original intention, I fancy, was to kill Ann Weston with that pistol, making it look like suicide. That was why you removed it from the scene of Aileen's murder, wasn't it?"

"No," said Bannister. "No! No! No!"

"Yes," said Rodericks firmly. "But Ann was so closely watched that you had no chance to use the pistol. They are, after all, nasty noisy things. Still, it wasn't very clever of you to use a poison which we can prove you had in your possession and which nobody else in the case could readily have got hold of. Of course, if it had worked you might — just possibly — have been all right. You would have come up with a story about Ann stealing the drug from your bag, I suppose."

"You can't prove any of this!"

"Wait and see," said Rodericks. His eyes twinkled, but there was a hard fierceness on his face. "You began to plan the murder a long time ago — once you were sure that Mrs.

Weston would turn to you for help and comfort in a time of distress. You had to put your plan into action before the date of Aileen's marriage in April. And then, when Carl Fleury returned eight days ago, there was even more need for haste. If Ann had eloped with him or married him suddenly, half the inheritance would have been irretrievably lost. Mrs. Weston knew about Carl Fleury — she told her husband about him and she told you as well. You had to act quickly. Mrs. Fitzpatrick's Valentine party seemed an ideal opportunity. You frightened the two girls last Thursday by following them home. And you frightened Ann Weston again on the Sunday. She thought there was something familiar about the man she saw in the shadows that night, by the way, but she failed to recognize you. The night before last you staged the fake break-in at this house. All this was done to establish the existence of an unknown molester. If it had worked out as you intended, the police would have found three dead bodies in this house. We would have spent our time fruitlessly trying to track down some tramp or psychopath. And, if by any chance, Dr. Weston had not died from the shock of finding his two daughters murdered, the trusty family doctor would have seen to it that he died shortly thereafter, and no suspicions would have been aroused. As a plan, it wasn't bad at all. It was in the small matter of implementation that you fell down so badly.

"Yesterday afternoon at five to six you telephoned here and asked for Mrs. Weston. You didn't expect she would be in because you knew she was going to lodge a complaint with the police. That's right, isn't it, Mrs. Weston?"

Lori looked up at Bannister. The doctor could not meet her gaze and his eyes roamed desperately around the room.

"Yes," Lori said in a clear, hard voice. "It was he who wanted me to go to the police. He even suggested that it would be best if I went just before six o'clock on my way to Molly's. So that there would be no risk of anyone finding out about it and telling my husband."

"And so that there would be only the two victims alone in the house. And so that Mrs. Weston, who was going to inherit all that lovely money, could not possibly be suspected. Oh, it was planned well." Rodericks addressed himself to the doctor again. "As soon as you knew that the two girls were alone you came around. Aileen must have been surprised to see you, but she let you in without question. You shot her but failed to kill her the first time. When you were forced to come back downstairs to finish your work, Ann Weston escaped. It was a good thing for her that you did not know the back gate was blocked with snow and could not be opened. You left the house, taking the revolver with you, and were back in your office in time to receive Mrs. Middleborough's telephone call."

"All guesswork," said Bannister desperately. "You can't prove a word of it."

"Unfortunately for you we can," the inspector replied. "You had a visitor during your absence. Mrs. Falls had been having trouble with her back. Since she was in Farnham anyway she decided to drop around to your office to consult you about it. But when she got there at six o'clock she found you were out. She rang your bell several times but could get no answer. She left then, and coming back past this house at five past six, she heard three shots. They were the first series of shots you fired at Aileen Weston."

Rodericks fished in his breast pocket and took out a sheaf

of typescript. He thumbed through it until he found what he wanted. "Yet when you made your initial statement to me yesterday you plainly said that you had been in your office from four o'clock on. You had sent your nurse home because there were some X-rays you wanted to look at. And you also said that your last patient had left by that time. Therefore I knew, even before I asked her, that Mrs. Falls could not have consulted you last night."

"I didn't answer the door!" said Bannister. He glared about him wildly, his lips drawn back in a snarl of rage and fear. Rodericks, who was listening for it, heard the note of hysteria in his voice. "It was the end of the day and I didn't want to see another patient. I heard her ring but I didn't answer the door."

"Your car was still in the driveway," Rodericks said, "but your lights were out. Do you generally read X-rays in the dark, Doctor? Perhaps it was lucky for Mrs. Falls that she didn't wait to see you return."

"The silly bitch," said Bannister viciously. "The silly whining bitch!"

At a nod from the inspector, Sergeant Peele reached out and seized the doctor by the left hand. There was a glint of metal, a click, and Bannister's wrists were handcuffed together. He stared down at them stupidly.

"George Bannister," said Rodericks formally, "I arrest you for the murder of Aileen Weston, and it is my duty to warn you that anything you say may be taken down and used in evidence at your trial."

"The silly bitch!" Bannister said again. "I wish she *had* waited. I'd have killed her too." He drew himself up and looked about him with a flash of pride and contempt. "The plan was brilliant. Absolutely brilliant. It's not my fault it failed. It was worth a gamble. You can't hang me."

"No," agreed Rodericks regretfully. "No, we can't hang you. If you are your usual charming self, you should be out in about ten years."

Corporal Moore and Constable Holmsted began to take the prisoner out to the car. He went with them dazedly, his shoulders slumped and his head down, but at the hall door he suddenly stopped and twisted half around so that he could see Rodericks. His face worked terribly as he tried to speak. When his voice came, it was hoarse, as though he had worn it out with shouting.

"The lights were on!" he gasped. "You tricked me, you bastard! I left the lights on! I'm sure I did!"

The outburst ended in a strangled sob. Corporal Moore gave him a push that spun him half around and sent him staggering towards the door. Rodericks stood where he was, his face impassive, until the front door slammed, then he glanced about him. Everyone looked shocked and subdued. Paul Anstruthers and Fred Dunn found their coats and hats and left without speaking. Carl Fleury helped Ann Weston into her coat.

"Bannister wasn't the only person who got into Ann's bedroom this afternoon," he said with a keen look at Rodericks. "Did you forget that? I got past your constable without being seen, and if I could do it so could someone else, presumably."

"That's right, sir," replied the inspector with a little smile that suddenly made him look sly. "Now that you mention it.

Perhaps it's as well I didn't think of it earlier though. Every little bit of pressure helps."

Fleury led Ann Weston away, and Mrs. Middleborough, who for once had nothing to say, tagged along behind them.

Lori Weston remained motionless in her chair. Inspector Rodericks fingered the piece of paper in his pocket and wished he had never chosen the police force as a career. At last he said, "I am afraid there is something else, Mrs. Weston."

She looked up at him and nodded listlessly. "It's Bob, isn't it?" she asked. "He's dead?"

Rodericks nodded. "I'm sorry."

He moved to the door and Sergeant Peele, after a last look at Lori, went with him. In the doorway Peele hesitated and stopped. His eyes asked the inspector a question.

"It will be a long, sad night," said Rodericks. "Stay if you want to, Ted."

Peele turned and went back, taking off his coat as he did so.

In front of the house were two police cars. Moore was sitting in the back seat of one of them with Bannister beside him. Constable Holmsted stood nearby. Rodericks spoke to Moore, "Take him into London and book him. Have him make a statement and sign it. There should be no difficulty about that now. I'll follow you in the other car, but I have to make a stop on the way." Then he turned to Holmsted, "I'll see you tomorrow morning in my office, Constable. At ten o'clock. I want to talk to you about Valentines, among other things."

The car bearing Moore and the prisoner moved off, wheels

spinning on the icy roadway. Rodericks stood on Maple Street and looked about him. A watery moon, nearly at the full, was rising behind the Carnegie library on the square. A few soft flakes of snow began to fall. Farnham looked as peaceful as a Christmas card.

Rodericks bent down and spoke to the driver of the second police car, "Go around by Hartmann's Corners, Constable. I have to stop in at the Falls' farmhouse."

It would be best to get Mrs. Falls' statement tonight, even although it was only confirmatory evidence now. It had not really been bluff, for he had known it must have happened that way he had described it. He had taken only one small gamble and that had been successful. Bannister, with his motive exposed and the evidence piling up against him, had momentarily been unable to remember whether he had left his consulting room lights on while he slipped out to commit murder. Still, Rodericks would be happier to have it all in writing with Mrs. Falls' signature on it.

He took out his pipe and filled it, then decided not to smoke it until he had had dinner. The beefsteak and kidney pie would be all gone, of course. He sighed, wondering what sort of supper his wife would be able to find for him when he finally got home.